TRULY MADLY MINE

J.H. CROIX

J.H. CROIX

Cover design by Najla Qamber Designs

Cover Photography: Reggie Deanching, R + M Photography, @RplusMphoto

Cover models: Michael Scanlon & Tionna Petramalo

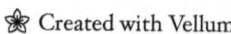 Created with Vellum

"Love never fails." ~ 1 Corinthians 13:8

Sign up for my newsletter for information on new releases & get a FREE copy of one of my books!

http://jhcroixauthor.com/subscribe/

Follow me!
jhcroix@jhcroix.com
https://amazon.com/author/jhcroix
https://www.bookbub.com/authors/j-h-croix
https://www.facebook.com/jhcroix
https://www.instagram.com/jhcroix/

Dani Love is the girl who got away. Actually, she dumped me.

Not exactly a stroke to my ego.

When I move back home, Dani is just as much *everything* as she was before. Maybe even more. Snappy and smart with an attitude for days. I want her, even if it's stupid.

Dani can't decide if it's better to ignore me, or fight with me. I'll fight and win. She just doesn't see it coming yet.

———

Wade Ellis is back. In *my* small town. I had it all figured out. Leave my past with Wade exactly where it belonged. The past stays in the past.

But Wade isn't getting my memo. He's ignoring every excuse I make.

His kisses are enough to literally set me on fire. Just when my defenses are burned to ash, I fess up to why I dumped him in the first place.

That should send him running. But no. Wade stole my heart once before, and now he seems determined to prove he's keeping it.

Chapter One

DANI

My hand slipped just as I brought down a bag of flour from the shelf above my head. The heavy bag bounced off another shelf and exploded, sending a cloud of flour all over me.

I opened my mouth to provide a choice curse—only to inhale a breath of flour. A coughing and sneezing fit ensued. When I finally caught my breath, I leaned against the wall with a sigh, not even bothering to deal with the torn bag of flour on the floor.

"Bless you," a voice said from the doorway.

Fuck my life.

Opening my eyes, I glanced down to see my apron and my hands and arms dusted white. Lifting a hand, I patted my hair, sending another cloud of flour into the air. I only hoped the flour I felt on my face obscured my blush when I lifted my eyes to meet the teasing gaze of Wade Ellis.

"Thanks," I said, instantly wishing my tone didn't come out so sharp. "Remind me whose idea it was to store the flour above my head."

Wade's grin stretched wider, and my pulse—rather disobedient, by the way—took off at a fast gallop. Meanwhile, a funny spinning feeling happened in my belly. There were many things I could control. The state of my body when Wade Ellis teased me was not one of them, despite my best efforts.

"Now that, I don't know for sure. But, this entire kitchen is definitely your domain, and you can be bossy. I'm bettin' it was your idea."

A little laugh broke loose. Because I couldn't help it. Even if I hated that Wade happened to find me in this state, I knew he was right. I *was* bossy and didn't mind owning it. I was certain I'd had a good reason for storing the flour there, but it seemed foolish now.

"What are you doing here so early this morning anyway?" I asked, glancing around for a towel.

My eyes landed on a stack of clean dish towels just by the door, and I pushed away from the wall to reach for one.

"I'm leading a long hike today," Wade replied. "Came by to stock up on some first aid supplies."

When I lifted my hand to brush the towel over my flour-covered hair, my bracelet caught on the elastic holding my ponytail in place. "Dammit," I murmured as I moved too quickly, almost yanking the elastic out.

Wade's low chuckle sent heat chasing over my skin like little licks of fire. "Hang on, let me help," he said, stepping closer.

My pulse went absolutely wild, my breath hitched in my throat, and a rush of heat blasted me from head to toe. I spent a lot of time *not* getting too close to Wade.

All that effort was wasted. He stood right at my side, his presence intense. He exhibited an easy strength and grace, no matter what he did. When I moved to try to untangle my bracelet, my elbow bumped into his muscled chest, and I almost cried out. Dear God, his chest was truly nothing but muscle.

My mouth did what it always did when I was around

Wade and started babbling. "Geez, dude. Working out enough?" I asked, my tone sarcastic.

I felt his hands carefully untangling a few curls in the elastic around my bracelet. "You know my job keeps me in shape," he murmured in reply. The contrast of his hard body and having this massive bear of a man carefully untangling my hair made my heart squeeze a little. "It's going to be easiest if I take it out."

I lowered my arms and waited, my curls falling in a wild tangle around my shoulders as he extricated the hairband. Wade finally stepped back, holding up the elastic. When I took it from him, my fingers brushed against his, sending a hot jolt of electricity up my arm.

We stood there, staring at each other. The normally busy staff kitchen at the lodge restaurant was quiet as dawn hadn't arrived. It wasn't even 5:30 a.m. yet. It felt as if Wade and I were all alone in the world, caught in this little bubble. The air felt as if it were firing sparks around us.

The usual teasing look in Wade's eyes faded as he searched my face. His espresso gaze darkened. A stillness fell over me as I looked at him, letting my eyes travel over the strong, clean lines of his face. Wade was *all* man, and tall with broad shoulders. His dark brows angled up slightly. His cheekbones were a thing of beauty—bold, sculpted curves that served to amplify his intense gaze. His perfectly straight nose was centered over his full lips. His square jaw had a shadow of stubble on it.

My fingers tingled with the urge to lift my hand and cup his cheek. I didn't know what the hell was going on with me. I couldn't seem to move. I was frozen, my breath coming in shallow little pants as I stared up at Wade. The space in the pantry was quiet for several long beats, but all the while, I could hear the rush of blood in my ears with every thump of my heart.

"Dani."

I heard my name on Wade's lips, but it had been years

since I'd heard that tone in his voice. It was rough and laced with need.

I felt caught in a current that spun into itself. The need to finally give in to what I'd been denying myself for years was so overpowering, I couldn't seem to call upon my snarky self and push back against it.

In a hot second, my head tipped back just as Wade leaned down. His lips brushed across mine when he murmured my name again, the whisper of his voice sending an electric tingle over my lips that raced through every cell in my body. I felt it course through me, sparking from the inside out.

A frayed sigh escaped me. Then, Wade fit his mouth over mine. One fiery second burned into another, everything going up in flames.

This wasn't the first time I had kissed Wade. Not even close. Our young, messy kisses in high school didn't hold a candle to this one. It was quite clear Wade had some practice in the years since then. He kissed me like he was born to do it—sensual strokes of his tongue against mine, his hand lacing into my hair as he angled my head to the side and devoured my mouth.

I wasn't passive. Oh no. I wanted this too much. Denial might've worked for a while—hell, even for years—but once the gates fell, all hell broke loose.

I was lost in the kiss. The feeling of his hands holding me against his strong, hard body was heady, and the taste of him was intoxicating. Sweet Jesus, his kiss set me on fire, inside and out.

"Hey Dani, do you—" The question stopped abruptly. "Oh! Oh my!"

The sound of footsteps hurrying away from the pantry echoed as Wade and I broke apart, our breath coming in sharp heaves.

Our eyes collided. Oh my God.

Chapter Two

WADE

Dani Love stared at me—her hair dusted with flour, those glorious curls bouncing around her shoulders as she shook her head. After a beat, her green eyes narrowed. Even with flour dusting her cheeks, the pink showed through. Her tongue swiped across her bottom lip.

"That was overdue," I finally said.

Dani's breath came out in a huff, and she put her hand on her hip and glared at me. "No, it was not."

"Before you start screaming at me, I've gotta go," I said flatly.

Dani blew out a puff of air, sending an errant curl out of her eyes. "Good," she said. "Please go."

For a moment, a retort was threatening to fly out. But I held back. Dani turned away, looking at the glimmer of sunrise beyond the pantry doorway through the window in the back of the kitchen. Her jaw was set, the lines of tension on her face so familiar.

I didn't know how, but I knew she was hurting. "Dani ..." I began.

Her gaze slid back to mine, her green eyes flashing. "Just

go, Wade. I know the group scheduled for the hike is waiting for you because that's why I'm here so early. They already had a quick buffet breakfast."

I wanted to kiss her again—this woman who was covered in flour, this woman who I'd loved since she was a girl.

Well, I couldn't say I loved her now. I wasn't too sure. I had once upon a time. She had dumped me, and life went on. I moved away and came back. For the last few years, we'd been in this seemingly endless cycle of sniping at each other.

Leaning over, she picked up the elastic that had fallen to the floor. "Have a good hike," she said. "I need to get cleaned up."

With that, she brushed past me, a little *zing* of electricity streaking up my arm where her elbow grazed against my forearm. Turning, I watched her hurry down the hall to the bathroom, her generous hips swaying with each quick step. I took a breath as the door closed behind her and let it out slowly. With a mental shake, I turned and headed to the front of the restaurant where I would meet the group for the hike.

Hours later, I leaned against a tree, scanning the vista in front of me. I was leading a group of eight on a winding hike through a pretty section of trail in the Blue Ridge Mountains. We were on the far side of Stolen Hearts Valley now. The nip of winter was strong in the air.

Technically, it was still autumn, but snow could fly within the next few weeks. The tree branches were stark against the sky. The famous blue haze lingered over the mountains and undulated ahead of us in the view.

Dani had been on my mind all day. I'd suspected for a long time there was something I was missing when it came to her and what happened between us years ago. Yet, I didn't know what the hell it was. I did know, with shocking clarity, that kissing Dani gave me a jolt I hadn't experienced since the last time I kissed her. Too long ago.

"Wade!" a voice called.

Glancing back, one of the men in the group was waving from where they had paused to rest for water and trail mix snacks. Adjusting my lightweight backpack, I strode over to them. "Yeah?"

The man who called over was an athletic type who was hiking with his wife as they marked off mountain ranges in their quest to spend time in every mountain range in the United States. They were retired and by no means young, but they were energetic and so full of joy it was a pleasure to have them in the group.

"How long to get back to the lodge?" he asked.

Glancing to my watch, I replied, "Two hours, give or take. It's usually quicker on the descent."

The man nodded, his eyes scanning the rest of the group. "Well, I say we get going, y'all. I'm ready for a good dinner back at the lodge, and a hot shower."

With that, we were headed back down. Along with the rest of the group, I was looking forward to a good dinner. Among the many perks of working at Stolen Hearts Lodge were the meals that came as part of the job.

Dani was the chef for the kitchen and managed the restaurant. Every night—with a few exceptions—Dani prepared a meal for employees in the staff section of the kitchen. We all usually piled in there if we had the time.

Except for that kiss this morning, the closest I felt to Dani since I returned to these mountains was when I was eating her meals. Cooking was practically spiritual for her. Everything she made was so damn good.

———

"Hey, mind passing me those potatoes?" I asked Dawson, who sat beside me at the crowded staff table in the back of the kitchen.

Dawson glanced at me, flashing a teasing grin. With an arch of his brow, he parried, "What'll you give me for them?"

I chuckled. "Not a damn thing." Looking toward Evie, his girlfriend who sat on his other side, I asked, "Evie, would you mind passing me those potatoes, please?"

Evie's brown ponytail swung as she shook her head and reached for the platter of rosemary and garlic seasoned potatoes. Ignoring Dawson, her blue eyes twinkled as she handed them to me. "Of course not," she chirped.

Dawson's gray gaze slipped to her. "Hey, I might as well not even be here."

Evie leaned over, brushing a kiss on his cheek. "You're here. It's just, Wade must be starving because I know they hiked ten miles today."

Dawson, easily assuaged by anything Evie said, slid an arm around her shoulders and dipped his head, pressing a lingering kiss to the side of her neck. Her cheeks were flushed pink when he lifted his head.

Dani happened to be approaching the table at that moment, and she glanced at Evie and Dawson. "You two need to get a room," she said pointedly.

I felt my eyes rolling before I even thought about it. "Oh really? You can't even handle a kiss," I countered.

Dani's eyes narrowed, and she thrust a platter of food at me. "I can handle a fucking kiss, Wade. Plus, in case it wasn't obvious, I wasn't talking to you."

I had reflexively reached for the platter and found myself holding a plate full of food while she spun around and stalked away. She walked swiftly to the front and pushed through the door into the restaurant kitchen, the hum of voices and the clatter of noise from the busy kitchen filtering through behind her.

Lucas, who happened to be sitting across from me, caught my gaze. "Well then. I'll take one of those if you don't mind," he said with a nod to the plate I held in my hand.

I gladly relinquished it and promptly started eating. Although Dani and I snapped at each other and teased with frequency, there was a bite to her frustration this evening. Just as I knew there was to mine.

I focused on my food, which was delicious, of course, and listened to the easygoing chatter as it carried on around me. I couldn't say why, but that little exchange with Dani didn't sit well with me.

After our dinner group filtered apart, I hung around, hoping to snag a chance to talk to her. I busied myself organizing supplies for our hiking groups in the back hallway where we stored first aid kits, prepackaged snack kits, and the like.

Hell if I knew what I meant to say, but it bothered me enough that I found myself searching her out a few hours later. I walked down the back hallway, when I knew the restaurant had closed and I would likely find her in her office. It wasn't quite as quiet as it had been this morning before sunrise, but all I could hear was the hum of the dishwasher and the low murmur of voices from the restaurant staff who'd stayed behind to clean up.

Dani's voice reached me as I walked down the hall. "I know, I know. I know you covered the last three Saturdays, but I'm hoping you don't mind," she said.

When I didn't hear the reply, I presumed she was on the phone with someone. Glancing at the clock mounted at the end of the hallway, I noted it was going on midnight. That meant Dani had been up for over eighteen hours at this point. Seeing as I was almost dead on my feet, I knew she had to be exhausted.

"Okay, that would be great," she said.

When I heard her say goodbye, I resumed walking, stopping to rest my shoulder on the doorframe.

Dani's back was to me where she stood, one hip leaning against her desk. Her hair was down, and she lifted her hand, smoothing it over her hair. To what end, I didn't know. Nothing could tame her wild brown curls. Once upon a time, I had loved to bury my hands in them.

A sharp, visceral memory of our kiss this morning pierced me—when I had her curls twined around my fingers for the first time in years—and set my body on fire all over again.

Dani dropped the phone on the desk and sighed.

"Working late as usual, I see," I said by way of greeting.

Dani turned, the ghost of a smile passing across her lips. All traces of the flour she'd spilled on herself this morning had been eliminated. She shrugged and replied, "Always. I could say the same for you."

Pushing off the doorframe, I stepped into her office. "Touché. Mind if I come in?"

The sharpness she carried earlier had softened. She shook her head, her curls bouncing around her shoulders. "Of course not."

The husky edge to her voice made my heart kick, good and hard, against my ribs. Stopping in front of her, I realized I hadn't thought through what I meant to say. I simply knew I wanted—no, *needed*—to talk to her.

My eyes landed on her freckles, sprinkled across her nose and cheeks. I'd never thought much about freckles, except I loved hers. Once upon a time, I tried to count them. She had giggled when I lost count.

Damn. It was crazy how much time could change things.

"I don't remember the last time I heard you giggle," I heard myself saying. I hadn't meant to speak my thoughts aloud, but there they were.

That single sentence hung in the air, bumping into everything else that crowded between us whenever Dani and I were in the same room together. Maybe it was because she was tired, but she didn't even snap at me. She lifted one shoulder in a shrug, turning and resting both hips against the desk as she eyed me.

"I laugh," she finally said, a familiar hint of defensiveness contained in her tone.

"I know you laugh. I said I hadn't heard you giggle. There's a difference."

Hell if I knew why I was debating the finer points of laughing versus giggling, but I was.

Dani wrinkled her nose, her mouth twisting to the side as she curled her hands over the edge of the desk. "How are they different?"

"Giggling is sillier."

She bit her lip, and I knew she was trying not to smile. "Somehow, I doubt that's what you wanted to talk about. What's your point, Wade?"

I took a breath, chasing down the tension building inside. "Look, I'm not sure what I said at dinner, but ..."

She gave her head a quick shake, cutting into my words. "You were joking. I get it."

Fuck it. I decided to stop dancing around the tangled history between us.

"Dani, what gives?"

"What do you mean?"

"You. Me. Us," I explained, gesturing back and forth between us. "Look, when I moved away, you lived your life and I lived mine. I came back, and it's like you're pissed off at me and you have been forever. In case you forgot this detail, you're the one who dumped me, not the other way around."

The lingering dull ache in my heart from our breakup throbbed, and I ignored it. I hadn't had much choice but to move on, so I had. It didn't mean I liked it.

Something flashed in her eyes—pain, anger, frustration, maybe all of those. Her gaze slid away from mine, and I heard her swallow. I scanned her face, the lines around her eyes, the set of her jaw, and the way her shoulders lifted slightly as she held herself stiffly.

"I know there's something there," I heard myself saying, a corner of my mind almost marveling I was saying anything at all. I was breaking the unspoken rule between us—never talk about the past, pretend like it didn't happen. The quickest way to get Dani to snap my head off was to keep barreling ahead when she had feelings. All kinds of feelings, from what I could ascertain.

She cleared her throat, turning back to face me. The pain flickering in her eyes for just a second took my breath away.

"I don't know what happened, but I hate seeing you like this." My voice came out gruff. Before I could think too hard about it, I acted on instinct, stepping closer and sliding my arms around her. For a beat, she tensed, but then she sighed and relaxed against me. Our kiss this morning in the early hours of dawn had been overdue, but somehow, holding her like this felt even more so.

Dani was warm and soft, and she smelled just like I remembered—a hint of sugar and vanilla because she was always baking. After a moment, I felt her hands loosen their grip on the desk and slide around my waist. Part of me was acutely aware this moment was as delicate as blown glass. It would shatter in a split-second if I did, or said, the wrong thing. Yet, another part of me savored it on such a bone-deep level that I couldn't let her go.

I breathed her in, savoring the feel of her. For once, she wasn't teasing as a way to keep me at a distance, or snapping at me to push me further away.

Dani was high-strung. Even when she was in a good mood, she didn't relax easily. After a few moments, I felt her shift away from my chest. Much as I didn't want to break free from her, or this moment, I wasn't going to push my luck.

Lifting my head, my heart squeezed like a clenched fist when I saw unshed tears glistening in her eyes.

Chapter Three

DANI

Looking up into Wade's familiar espresso gaze, tears stung my eyes, and I worried I might burst out crying. I managed a shallow breath and swallowed, a wobbly effort to get my emotions under control.

"Dani," Wade said, the tender rasp in his voice nearly undoing me.

I couldn't figure out how we had gotten to this point. I had been doing so well, so spectacularly well, at avoiding this. He lifted a hand, his thumb brushing across my cheek. I hadn't even realized a tear had fallen.

His forehead fell to mine as he murmured, "I don't know what it is, but I'm sorry."

His lips brushed across mine—once, twice, three times. When he straightened and raised his head, the urge to lean up and kiss him again was almost overpowering. I managed to keep myself in check, but just barely.

The tenderness contained in his gaze yanked at my heartstrings. I scrambled for purchase inside my heart and mind. There was a reason I had resisted letting myself get close to Wade. I felt his gaze searching mine, and I sensed he wanted to ask what was bothering me.

I prayed he wouldn't. The young man Wade had once been knew me in ways no one else did. Perhaps it had been a few years, and perhaps he didn't know me the way he once did, but he gave me the space I needed right now.

"I don't know when," he said softly, "but we need to talk."

I opened my mouth to reply, only to hear footsteps coming quickly down the hallway.

"Hey Dani, do you know—?" Shay Martin appeared in the doorway, literally skidding to a stop when she saw Wade and me. "Oh, sorry!" She backed away and dashed down the hall.

Wade stepped back when she appeared, and now a foot or so separated us. It felt like miles and miles, a chasm I didn't know how to cross.

"I have to go," I said abruptly, before turning and almost running down the hallway.

Only when I burst through the door into my studio cabin, with cold air whooshing around me, did I realize I didn't have my jacket and I'd left my purse behind in the office.

Good thing I lived on the premises at Stolen Hearts Lodge in one of the staff cabins. Also, a good thing I never bothered locking my door.

Just now, I couldn't face Wade again, no matter how ridiculous it was that I left him behind in my own office.

———

The staff kitchen was quiet when I entered the following morning, and I breathed a sigh of relief. Managing the restaurant staff and most of the lodging for the hotel here meant my days were filled with people. Stolen Hearts Lodge was a high-end outdoor resort tucked into the Blue Ridge

Mountains in Stolen Hearts Valley, North Carolina. The owners, Jackson and Ash Stone, a brother and sister who had grown up here on their family's old farm had renovated it into what it was now.

Of late, Jackson was the only one around, what with Ash traipsing around the country with her boyfriend on the rodeo circuit. I'd known Jackson and Ash in high school and jumped at the chance to take the chef position here. When I realized how little Jackson enjoyed managing anything, I had largely taken over most of that role for the last few years. His girlfriend, Shay, the very woman who encountered me in Wade's arms last night, had been a huge help lately, assuming most of the management for the rescue program and veterinary clinic that were another part of this massive operation.

Recalling the moment Shay saw Wade and me last night had heat blooming on my cheeks. Although, I didn't have to worry about Shay gossiping. She had swiftly become a good friend and also understood how painful rumors could be, more so than most.

I checked the office, laughing softly to myself when I realized Wade had closed the door for me after I bolted. My jacket was draped haphazardly on my chair where I had left it and my purse was still on the desk. When my eyes landed on my phone, where I dropped it on a stack of papers, I lifted it to see a text from Wade.

Closed up for ya. Next time, try to run out a little faster. ;)

Emotions welled in my chest and my lips tugged into a smile. Wade was good at getting me to laugh.

I plugged my phone in and did my usual loop, striding through the staff kitchen, and into the restaurant kitchen. At this hour, it was quiet and sparkling clean, just as expected.

The front of the restaurant was lovely this time of day, nothing more than a glimmer of sunrise above the mountains in the distance through the front windows. The restaurant was housed in a massive old barn. It had been renovated down to the original beams and was now an upscale, charming space. The restaurant took up half of the bottom floor and stayed busy all the time.

We had guests traipsing in and out of the luxury rooms on the upper floor. Another nearby renovated barn was entirely for guest lodging. In addition, there were high-end studio cabins scattered throughout the nearby trees, along with some set aside for staff lodging.

The original part of the farm where the old family farm-house was situated had a new barn built into a sloping hill. The lower floor of that barn housed horses, while the upper floor was used for administrative offices and the vet clinic, which Jackson ran.

Another barn in that area was where they ran Stolen Hearts Rescue, an animal rescue program for a hodgepodge of animals. They rescued everything from the usual dogs and cats to pigs, horses, chickens, goats, and more. Jackson also helped lead the first responder team for Stolen Hearts Valley Emergency Response.

I paused by the windows that looked out over the valley, smiling softly at the hint of light shimmering behind the mountains. When the sun broke through, it would fall through these windows in shafts, gleaming on the wide plank hardwood floors.

With it still mostly dark outside, I flicked the lights on, letting my gaze scan the restaurant. The wooden tables were clean and already set with simple white cloth napkins and silverware. The team last night had left everything as it should be for the morning shift. I prided myself on running a tight ship, and I loved my staff. They were like family.

Satisfied, I turned and headed back into the kitchen. The morning crew would be here within an hour, and mean-while, I had baking to begin. With my priorities in order, I started a pot of coffee—dark, exactly how I liked it. After that, I went to fetch flour from the pantry, pleased Evie had already re-organized the shelves at my request and put the flour on a lower shelf.

Of course, recalling my little flour fiasco yesterday morning sparked heat inside of me. Because I couldn't think about that without thinking about Wade's kiss. Just my luck, one of my favorite things to do—baking—was now linked to Wade.

More specifically, flour was linked to Wade. Seeing as I couldn't bake without flour, well, you get my point. Forcibly shoving Wade out of my mind—conveniently, I'd had years of practice at that—I returned to the staff kitchen where I did all of my baking.

With quiet surrounding me, I poured myself a cup of coffee and got to work. I was kneading a batch of dough when the door to the back hallway opened. I tensed instantly, anxious it was Wade. Here's the fucking kicker. I was disappointed when I looked over my shoulder and saw it wasn't him.

Shay walked through the door, knocking the snow off her boots as she stepped inside. Shaking her jacket, she hung it on the hooks by the door and glanced over at me.

"It's snowing," she announced.

She walked a straight line across the kitchen to the coffee pot on the counter. The counter was parallel to the large stainless-steel table running through the center of the kitchen where I was working.

"It is? It wasn't snowing when I came in." Pausing, I took a sip of my coffee before continuing to knead the dough.

Shay spun around with a mug in hand and walked to the table, where she slid her hips on one of the stools across from me. Her dark-blonde hair was damp and fell around her shoulders. Her green eyes were bright as she smiled over at me. After taking a long swallow of her coffee, she sighed. "Delicious. I'm always glad you make the first pot of coffee around here."

"How come?" I asked as I rolled the dough into an oval

and dropped it in a glass bread pan rubbed with olive oil. I immediately shifted to the next ball of dough waiting for me to knead it.

"Because you always make it dark. I'm not complaining about anyone else who makes it, but yours is the best."

I grinned. "Well, I won't argue that point. I can't stand half-ass coffee."

Shay's eyes flicked to the small bowls of ingredients beside me on the table. "What kind of bread are you making?"

"Rosemary, garlic, and feta."

"Oh my God, that is going to be *so* good. When will the first loaf be out of the oven?"

"First, it needs time to rise, so it won't be ready for three hours at least."

Shay beamed. "Perfect. I'll take a break and come get some fresh bread. I'll need one by then. I'm redoing the whole website for the rescue program, and it's a little tedious."

"Thank God you're doing that. It probably hasn't been updated since Ash threw it together a few years ago."

Shay laughed softly. "Considering that websites aren't really Ash's thing, she did a good job for something totally basic. And then, Jackson did nothing after that. Honestly, I should've gotten to it sooner, but ..."

Her words trailed off when I laughed. "You've only had a million and one things to do. Jackson let just about every-thing slide on the business end before you got here. If I haven't mentioned it lately, thank God you're here."

Shay shrugged lightly. "I'm just so glad to be here."

"And, head over heels in love with Jackson, who's into you like nobody's business," I teased.

A flush washed over Shay's cheeks. I didn't realize I had opened myself up for a return volley until she spoke. "Speaking of head over heels, what did I interrupt last night?"

I knew my own cheeks were pink, and I bit back a sigh. "Nothing," I muttered, grabbing my coffee and draining it. Restless, I paused in my kneading and dusted my hands on my apron as I quickly rounded the table to refill my coffee cup.

When I returned, Shay was waiting patiently. "That wasn't nothing. I might not have been around here too long, but there has *always* been something with you and Wade. And Jackson told me y'all actually dated in high school."

After another gulp of coffee, I started kneading again, relieved I had something to do with my hands. "Fine. So, we did. Date in high school, that is."

"So, did something happen again? I'll be honest, it's obvious you two like each other. Half the time, you're all bitchy with him, and he dishes it right back. But, I see the way he looks at you, and I see how hard you try not to look at him."

Although I had only gotten to know Shay well in the last year, she had become a good friend. She'd grown up in the area like me, but I hadn't known her too well when we were younger. I wanted to hedge and avoid this conversation, but it didn't seem fair. I finally looked up and met her eyes. Although there was a teasing glint in them, it faded when she saw me. I didn't know what she saw reflected in my own, but she set her coffee down.

"Okay, I was just teasing. It seems like I hit on a sore subject, huh?"

I looked back down at the dough, rolling it into a tidy ball and putting it in another oiled pan. "Yeah, we have history. I'm not exactly sure what you mean about the way Wade looks at me, but it's kind of complicated."

Shay was quiet for a moment before she said, "People are complicated. When I saw you two last night, it was the first time I've ever seen you that relaxed. I mean, not to be weird, but it seems to me like you matter to each other. Perhaps a lot."

A jolt of emotion rocked me. I viscerally remembered the sensation of being held in Wade's strong arms last night. Wade did matter to me. *A lot.* Just as Shay observed. But if he ever knew why I broke up with him and what happened, he might never forgive me.

I reached for another ball of dough, hoping Shay didn't pick up on my emotional state. "Nothing is simple when it comes to Wade and me." When I looked across the table at her, her mouth twisted to the side, her gaze considering as she regarded me.

"So what? Look, take it from someone with a totally fucked-up and complicated past. If someone is the right person for you, don't let that shit get in the way."

"You don't understand," I protested. Even to me, my tone sounded feeble.

She took a long, slow sip of her coffee before responding. "I'm not saying I understand, not specifically. But generally speaking, I *do*. I don't know what the deal is, but I think you're getting in your own way."

Chapter Four

WADE

"Oh yeah, this oughta be fun," Jackson muttered under his breath.

Sliding my gaze to his, I fought the urge to grin. I worked with Jackson on Stolen Hearts Emergency Response Team, and we'd just been called out to a rather epic and ridiculous situation.

"You fucking asshole!" Sarah Lind shouted from below the porch.

Unfortunately for Sarah, the porch in question was built on angled beams jutting out over a cliff. It offered an excellent view of the valley, with a small brook bubbling in the trees nearby.

Lyle Smith shouted back to her. "For fuck's sake, Sarah! Now *really* isn't the time."

"Oh, I'd say now *is* the time!" Doreen Smith, Lyle's wife, called from where she stood nearby, taking turns glaring at Sarah and Lyle.

Glancing to the police officer with us, I asked, "Do you want to deal with Doreen and Lyle while we figure out how the hell to get Sarah out of this mess?"

The police officer let out a sigh. "Sure. At the moment, I envy your job."

Jackson chuckled. "Well, let's all hope Lyle learns how to keep it in his pants after this."

Lyle happened to be approaching and heard that last comment. "No need for your commentary, Jackson," Lyle said sharply.

The police officer turned to Lyle, leveling him with a pointed glare. "Lyle, right now, this mess is entirely of your making."

Lyle's cheeks flushed a deep shade of red. He ran a hand through his hair and sighed. "I know, for fuck's sake. Do you guys have any idea how to get her down?" he asked, gesturing toward Sarah, who hung from the deck over the cliff. She actually had on a harness. Not for climbing, mind you.

"In all seriousness, can you please tell us what happened?" the police officer asked.

As Jackson and I suited up in our climbing gear, Lyle launched into an explanation. In short, he and Sarah had been having some early-morning fun in a sex swing. A sex swing that apparently belonged to Doreen, his wife. Doreen was supposed to be out of town, but she returned home early. Now, here we were.

"Dude, how the hell did Sarah end up hanging off the porch?" I mused to Jackson as we looked up at her.

Jackson shook his head. "I don't know that I want to know. I think it had something to do with Doreen."

Humor helped in trying situations, especially when no one's life was at risk. While Sarah was definitely in an awkward position, she would be fine, albeit probably a bit cold.

"All right, let's climb on up," I said as I eyed the steep cliff underneath the porch. "We'll put her in a climbing harness and lower her down."

This porch was in such poor condition, we assessed it was better for us to rescue Sarah from the cliff below rather than from the porch itself. Not that she was at risk of falling, but we estimated having the weight of all three of us on it wasn't the smartest move. After this rescue happened, Jackson and I would be recommending to the town that they request this deck be demolished.

The Appalachian Mountains were filled with cabins tucked in odd locations, some built more safely than others. This one was definitely on the questionable side.

It didn't take long for us to fetch Sarah from her predicament. Once she was down on the ground, safe and sound, and we medically cleared her, she started a fight. As it was, Jackson and I had to help the police officer break up a small scuffle between her and Lyle. Doreen attempted to enter the fray, apparently happy to take sides with Sarah over what a scumbag Lyle was.

We learned Sarah had ended up on the porch when Lyle locked her out to try to hide her presence from Doreen. Seeing as there were plenty of windows, his attempt failed. Doreen stormed the deck. In the ensuing argument, Sarah, who was naked and in a harness, shoved Lyle or Doreen—that detail remained unclear—and was shoved in return. She tripped over a flimsy deck chair and the railing broke when she fell against it. The harness tangled on the broken railing, and there she was, in her undignified escape.

Our escapade ended with the police officer calling for backup. Although Jackson and I could help break up a fight, we didn't have the authority to arrest. After that little mess was over, I looked at Jackson in the truck. "I need a beer, and I'm fucking starving."

Jackson grinned, his blue eyes crinkling at the corners as he ran a hand through his messy brown curls. "Right there with you, buddy. Let's hit up Lost Deer Bar, whaddya say?"

"Where else?"

"Mind if I make a quick call?" he asked as I started driving.

"Of course not."

A few seconds passed before he said, "Hey, babe."

The moment he said that, I knew he was calling Shay. If you had told me a year ago Jackson would fall in love, I would've laughed. Now, Shay, his best buddy's little sister, stole Jackson's heart so fast, I had actually worried for his sanity for a bit there.

Shay was the best thing that had ever happened to Jackson. At least, as far as I could tell.

"Yeah. Wade and I are going to grab a beer and some dinner at Lost Deer. Are you hungry?"

There was a pause as he listened to her reply and then moved the phone away from his mouth just as I came to a stop before turning onto the highway. "Mind if Shay and some of the others meet us there?"

"'Course not," I replied, turning onto the road that would lead us to the bar in question.

"See you in a bit. Love you." Jackson hung up.

That was how bad he had it. The man told Shay he loved her probably about ten times a day in my presence when I happened to be around them.

In that vein, I felt the need to chime in. "You know, I gotta tell ya, I'm damn glad you got over yourself with Shay."

Jackson chuckled. "Not that I have much choice. That woman slays me," he said with bold honesty.

We fell quiet for a few moments. The sky was stained pink and lavender with a dusting of snow on the mountain ridge ahead. It didn't snow all winter in the Blue Ridge Mountains, but enough to give the mountains a bit of that fairy dust every year with occasional heavier snows.

Jackson's voice broke into the quiet. "Speaking of women, Shay mentioned she walked in on a moment between you and Dani."

I silently swore. Not that Shay was much of a gossip, at all, but I should've expected her to say something to Jackson. Dani would lose her fucking mind though. Nosy as she could be about others, and as freely as she poked fun at herself about many things, Dani was fiercely private in some areas of her life. Romance, or anything resembling it, was one of those areas.

Frankly, in the several years since I had returned to Stolen Hearts Valley after spending some time out West, I had no idea if she'd even dated anyone. I had no problem admitting I was quite curious.

As I turned the steering wheel into the parking lot at Lost Deer Bar, I glanced over at Jackson. "What the hell did Shay tell you?"

I could tell Jackson was fighting a grin, and I looked away, shaking my head. I spotted a parking spot in the far corner and aimed over in that direction.

"She said she was pretty sure she walked in on you two kissing. That's it. Dude, you know she won't say anything to anyone else."

Jackson knew Dani maybe as well as I did, so he knew that would matter to her. "I know she won't. It's just, Dani will be fucking pissed. Not with Shay, but with the situation." I rolled to a stop and put the truck in park before cutting the engine.

"So, what gives?" Jackson asked.

I leaned my head against the seat and let out a gusty sigh. "Hell if I know. It's no secret there's tension between Dani and me. If I had my way, we'd get that shit out of our systems."

Jackson chuckled. "I can imagine. You know, far as I know, she's never dated anyone since you two were together in high school. Last thing I recall was her throwing that slushy at you in the cafeteria."

I remembered the slushy, but I couldn't focus on that point. A little shock jolted me as I swiveled my head to look at Jackson. "You're fucking kidding me," I said flatly. "I figured she was just keeping things quiet."

Jackson lifted a shoulder in an easy shrug. "Maybe, but I don't think so. Not that people tell me everything, but I don't know how she could keep something like that a secret for too long."

"That can't be true," I muttered.

"How the hell would you know?" Jackson countered. "You went to college out West, and she stayed here. You only moved back a few years ago."

"Look, this thing with Dani is complicated," I began.

"I don't see what's so fucking complicated. You totally have a thing for her, so do something about it."

It all sounded so simple coming from Jackson. Pocketing my keys, I rolled my eyes when I looked his way again. "Right. Like it was that easy for you and Shay."

"Yeah, and you made sure I stayed on the right track. Just returning the favor," he replied, clapping me on the shoulder before he climbed out of the truck.

Moments later, we were weaving our way through the tables in Lost Deer Bar. This place was a local favorite, and on the circuit for bands on the winding roads that led to Nashville. Tonight, a duo was playing on the stage in the back.

Jackson and I made our way over to the restaurant side of the bar. This bar had been around as long as I could remember. It had started in a small home, just a tiny mom-and-pop kind of place. It had expanded significantly since then, with the original area nothing more than a waiting section.

A massive rectangular building had been added and had one side with small circular tables and the stage, with the other side offering larger dining tables and booths. A wide bar ran the length of the entire space in the back. Scuffed hardwood floors and simple wooden tables completed the low-key décor. They served damn good pub fare and had excellent beer, produced through an offshoot of the family's business, the Lost Deer Winery & Brewery.

"You grab a table, I'll grab us a pitcher of the house draft," I said, leaning toward Jackson so he could hear me.

At his nod, I veered toward the bar in the back. I scanned the area, expecting to find Delilah Carter. Delilah was an old friend and the regular bartender here. She was nowhere to be found, so when Abe, who filled in occasionally, leaned his elbows on the glossy wooden bar, I asked, "No, Delilah?"

Abe grinned. "Nah, man. Remy's sister, Shay, hooked Delilah up with a free ski trip to Alaska. So, she took off. That girl deserves a vacation like nobody's business. Don't tell me you have a thing for her," he said, a sly look entering his gaze.

I threw my head back with a laugh. "Nah. She's just a friend and I wondered where she was."

"Seeing as she works all the damn time, everyone's wondering where she is. Anyway, what can I get for you?"

"I'll take a pitcher of the house draft and four glasses," I said, figuring at least two more people would want some beer.

Within a few minutes, I was taking a swallow of my beer and leaning back in my seat at the booth Jackson had commandeered in the far corner. "Let's hope not too many people show up," I said, glancing at him.

"I know. All the tables were taken. First come, first serve. The rest can fend for themselves," Jackson teased.

A waitress paused by the table. "Are you boys eating now, or waiting?"

"We're starving, and we're not waiting," Jackson said bluntly.

I grinned. We ordered burgers and fries and settled in. Before our food arrived, I heard Dani's voice. It was incredible I could hear her over the voices carrying on around us and the music in the background. But then, that was the effect Dani Love had on me.

For the last few years, I'd respected the boundary she'd drawn between us. A boundary reinforced with snipes, glares, icy stares if I pushed too hard, and distance, plenty of cold distance. After our kiss and the vulnerability I saw seeping through, there was no way in hell I could go back to that.

Turning, I saw her approaching with Shay and Valentina, and Lucas strolling in behind them. Shay had her own kind of beauty—that honey blonde hair, sweet curvy body, and flashing green eyes. She did nothing for me. Not that I was trying to look, because I respected my friends, but it was more of an objective experiment to test myself.

Next, I let my eyes slide to Valentina. She was the kind of woman who turned heads. Her deep-red hair was like a flame in the crowded room, making it difficult not to notice her. She had her curls pulled up in a ponytail that cascaded down her back. With freckled skin and wide blue eyes, she was the kind of woman who brought men to their knees. Not me. Hell no. All I had was appreciation. A damn good thing for that. I was quite certain Lucas would kick any man's ass who looked too long and hard at Valentina. He was so whipped over her.

The moment my eyes landed on Dani, it was like lightning struck me, electrifying every cell in my body. Dani, with her brown curls and pretty green eyes. She had a girl-next-door beauty to her. Now, *she* did a hell of a lot more than nothing to me. On the short side, she laughed at something Lucas said right before they reached our table.

I wanted her to smile at me like that—not that she was smiling at Lucas in a romantic way. But there was an openness to her, and none of the history that crowded between us was in her eyes.

I'd felt so damn lost when she broke up with me back in high school. I never knew why. I figured I had to just let it go. But now, I was determined to find out what happened and banish whatever it was that caused her pain.

She hadn't even noticed I was there when she slid her hips onto the bench seat and started scooting over. Her curls bounced when she turned toward me, her eyes widening slightly. For a beat, she froze.

Much to my satisfaction, Valentina said, "Scoot, scoot, Dani."

Dani didn't have much choice, not without making it obvious she didn't want to sit beside me. Dani scooted closer and Valentina sat down beside her, with Shay sitting opposite Dani and Lucas directly across from Valentina.

These booths were really designed for four people. Six made it crowded. But I wasn't about to complain about the fact that I could feel Dani's warm heat pressing against mine by virtue of us being crammed in here.

Shay pressed a kiss to Jackson's cheek before looking over at me. "Hey, Wade, I hear y'all had a fun call today."

"Do tell," Lucas said as he reached across the table and curled his hand around Valentina's. Like I said, he was whipped.

"Oh, it was definitely one of the more fun ones we've had in a while. Only reason we were there was because Sarah got shoved off the porch by Doreen. Well, sort of," I explained.

"That was after Lyle tried to hide Sarah out there because they were, uh, busy in the bedroom in the sex swing. Doreen wised to where Sarah was, and all three of them got into it on the porch. Sarah fell when the railing broke," Jackson added helpfully.

"It's freezing out today," Valentina said, her blue eyes widening as she leaned over to look at me.

Jackson chuckled. "Damn straight. By the end of it all, Doreen and Sarah were duking it out with Lyle. They were on the same team by that point. We had to help break up the fight and wait for backup so the police could arrest all three of them."

Shay grinned and Dani giggled beside me, the sound spinning around my heart. As if she realized what I meant by my comment last night, her eyes swung up to mine, a faint pink blush staining her cheeks.

"Here's your food, guys," our waitress said, breaking through the moment.

The waitress took orders for the rest of the table, and conversation moved on. There was nothing unusual about this night. Since I'd been back in Stolen Hearts Valley, working at the lodge with Dani, I'd spent many a night with her and friends, chatting casually and keeping my distance. I only kept my distance because it was crystal clear that was what she wanted. I managed my frustration with that situation by teasing her every chance I got.

Tonight was different. Although I didn't let it show and managed to keep up my end of the conversation whenever it was lobbed in my direction, half of my attention was always on Dani. It didn't help matters one bit to have her scent—sugar and vanilla—winding around me, or to know her soft, lush curves were only inches away. I had to resist the urge to slide my arm around her shoulder. I didn't. I knew that would be pushing it too far.

Chapter Five

DANI

Ducking my head and stuffing my hands in my pockets, I walked through the trees toward my small studio cabin. The thin layer of snow on the ground crunched under my feet, and I shivered slightly when a gust of wind blew through the valley.

Despite the cold outside, I felt like I was on fire inside. Spending a few hours mashed up beside Wade in the bar had driven me to near insanity. Somehow, that silly moment when I dumped flour all over myself in the pantry had blown open the door I'd been trying to keep closed and locked ever since Wade moved back to Stolen Hearts Valley.

Hell, the door didn't just blow open, it fell off the damn hinges. I couldn't say what had shifted. Except, in that moment, my guard had fallen just enough that I kissed Wade.

Fuck my life. All my efforts to hold my feelings at bay now felt futile.

I'd been so damn cocky to think I had the situation in hand. Maybe I could get a hold of it again. The problem was I didn't know if I wanted to anymore.

The banked embers inside had been kicked loose and the heat contained within them exploded into flames. The temptation to give into it, to finally let myself have what I told myself I couldn't even want, was almost overwhelming.

"Dani!"

Wade's voice reached me through the trees. The moment I heard it, my heart stumbled, tripped, and fell, and my belly spun in wild flips.

Keep walking. Just go back to your cabin and ...

My body, quite willful at the moment, boldly ignored my attempt at lecturing myself. My feet stopped, and I turned to look back. The staff cabins were scattered in the trees out behind the main guest barn for Stolen Hearts Lodge. Several winding paths led to the cabins. During winter, holiday lights were strung through the trees, adding a festive touch to the walk home.

Because I knew where everyone was—seeing as I was the one in charge of getting new staff situated when they came here—I knew perfectly well that Wade's cabin was close to mine. But just far enough that I could try to ignore his presence most of the time.

Instead of angling up the short path leading off this one to his place, he strolled quickly through the trees toward me, his arms swinging easily. I doubted he was bothered by the cold. Wade was like a personal heater. I remembered what it felt like to be wrapped in his warm, strong embrace when I was younger.

A shaft of fierce longing struck me. Oh my God. The need to relax and just let myself fall into what I knew would feel so good with Wade was like a tide rolling over me and catching me in its current.

Wade stopped in front of me, his eyes meeting mine in the dim light cast from the holiday lights. "You're cold," he said by way of greeting.

It just so happened that I shivered unconsciously when

he stopped in front of me. I nodded, seeming incapable of getting a grasp on actual words.

His eyes searched my face, and then he was sliding his hand around my shoulders, turning and guiding me swiftly along the path. "Let's get you inside. What you're wearing doesn't even count as a winter jacket," he murmured.

Normally, I would have some sort of argumentative retort. I had to scramble for one, finally replying, "You know, I'm perfectly capable of walking on my own."

My tone was a little snippy, and I didn't care. In fact, I was a little relieved to feel that side of myself rise up again. I was forever annoyed with myself for my lingering feelings for Wade.

His low chuckle sent a prickle chasing down my spine. Every sensation connected to him sprinkled fuel into the fire burning inside me.

"As if I didn't know that," he countered as he opened the door to my cabin.

Without thinking, I stepped through the door, spinning back at the last minute. "What are you doing, Wade?"

"We need to talk," he said flatly. He didn't even wait for me to invite him in, stepping in behind me and closing the door shut. He leaned against it, hooking one hand in the pocket of his jeans.

That familiar defensiveness, which had served me so well when it came to Wade, flexed its muscles. "About what?" I snapped.

Not waiting for him to reply, I knocked the snow off my boots and kicked them off before hanging up my jacket and striding across my cabin to turn up the heat. Most of the cabins were similar, and those that staff lived in were all studio-sized. The front door opened into a main room with a bench and hooks for jackets by the door, a queen-size bed in one corner, and an efficiency kitchen in the other corner. There was a small round table and a few chairs to create the impression that one had an actual dining room. On the opposite side of the bed was a door that led into a bathroom.

Although they were small, the cabins were quite luxurious. With a high ceiling to let lots of light in through the front windows, the floors were glossy hardwood, and the furnishings were simple, but elegant—lightweight, modern wooden furniture with airy fabrics. The bathroom was pure luxury, with a large tub and shower.

After adjusting the thermostat, I turned back to find Wade still waiting. Part of me didn't want to cross the room and get closer to him again. Proximity to Wade at this juncture seemed insane.

Yet, I didn't want to be a coward. I certainly didn't want Wade to sense how jumpy I felt around him. I was nothing if not stubborn though. Steeling myself inside, I crossed the room, stopping in front of him. I was so rattled by my body's reaction—as if an engine were revving inside of me—I was acutely aware of ensuring I was far enough away that I didn't accidentally reach out and touch him.

As if *that* could be an accident.

Resting a hand on my hip, I cocked my head to the side. "Well?"

Wade's gaze darkened as he looked at me. My nipples— damn my nipples—puckered inside my bra and I suddenly regretted taking my jacket off. I wore a thin cotton shirt underneath. There was nothing special or sexy about it. And yet, I felt his eyes flick down and knew he could see my nipples perking up at his attention.

I tried to take a breath, but got nothing more than a shallow sip of air. My pulse skittered off and that inconvenient heat prickled over the surface of my skin.

"We need to talk about why the hell you've been so mad at me ever since I came back, and what happened yesterday."

I didn't know how it was possible, but my pulse kicked up a notch. He touched on topics I had zero interest in discussing. Denial was a very effective coping skill, and I'd relied on it heavily in dealing with Wade the last few years.

Swallowing, I stared at him. I didn't even bother to try to formulate an answer. With the hum of anticipation fuzzing my thoughts and butterflies twirling in my belly, I knew I couldn't think clearly. Much less come up with any kind of reasonable answer.

"I don't want to talk, Wade," I finally said.

A crease formed above his brow. Although his posture remained relaxed where he leaned against the door, I could see the subtle tension enter his body. His shoulders stiffened a bit and his jaw clenched slightly as he held my gaze.

"Dani, you never told me why you dumped me in high school. I let it ride. But I'm done. This thing between us isn't over, and you can stop bothering to pretend like it is."

A flash of anger pierced me, the heat of it spinning into the fire already burning me up inside. I didn't even realize I had moved until I was standing right in front of him, pointing my finger at his chest.

"You don't get to *make* me talk about anything, Wade."

I knew I was overreacting, and I knew I was being defensive. I prided myself for not being an asshole. But the lingering guilt I carried for never explaining why I broke up with him had been eating at me for too freaking long.

"Maybe I can't make you talk about anything," Wade countered, "but I have every right to try. Also, you're the one who kissed me first yesterday."

My heart was thrashing wildly in my chest, and I felt the slick heat building between my thighs. Oh, I could admit it. Wade was hot. *Seriously* hot. Even worse, he kissed like a dream.

That inconvenient detail revved me like nothing else did. It was a pedal on the gas in my body's engine. With nothing but emotion driving me, I stepped closer, my hand falling to his chest. It was hard, and I could feel the rapid thump of his heartbeat against my palm.

I opened my mouth to say something else. Nothing came out other than a little hitch of my breath in the back of my throat. Wade said something that didn't even register to me, and then his hand was sliding into my hair as he fit his mouth over mine.

Chapter Six

DANI

I heard the low moan escape my throat when Wade's tongue swept into my mouth, and I didn't even care. He drew back slightly, one of his hands lacing into my hair as he murmured my name and angled my head to deepen our kiss. His other hand slid down my spine to cup my bottom and pull me fast against him where I could feel the hard ridge of his arousal. I truly didn't care about anything except this.

This being the feel of Wade, strong and hard against me. The scent of him—woodsy with a hint of snow clinging to him—wrapped around me and invaded all my senses like a drug.

The feel of his kiss—slow, deliberate, sensual, and deep—was so overwhelming, I simply tumbled into it. This was everything, everything I had tried to deny myself for too damn long.

I flexed into him, plastering my body against his. The man he was now was all strong, hard, honed planes. Being held by him felt so right that all I could do was surrender to it.

When I moaned again, his lips broke from mine, and he

dusted hot kisses along my jawline. His teeth caught the lobe of my ear lightly, sending an intense shiver through my entire body. Little nips along the sensitive skin on my neck had me trembling against him, my hips rocking into the cradle of his.

"Dani." The sound of my name in his gruff voice elicited a whimper from me.

I barely recognized myself. I was awash in sensation and need, and Wade was the only person who could assuage it.

I ran my hand over his chest, savoring the hard planes and the ripple of his abdomen as I stroked across it before I cupped my palm over the hard length of his cock. A rush of satisfaction came when I felt him swell slightly under my touch.

"Fuck, Dani," he growled, his teeth grazing along my neck again with a light nip as I rocked my hips over his thigh when his knee slid in between my legs.

A piercing streak of pleasure raced through me. His hand was sliding down to cup my breast with his thumb and forefinger lightly pinching my nipple through my T-shirt.

"Wade, please." I gasped when he pressed his knee against me again, sending another hot jolt of pleasure spinning from my core.

Suddenly, he stilled, lifting his head slowly. He didn't move, but I could feel the tension nearly vibrating through his body. My eyes opened to find his gaze waiting—intent, dark, and searching.

I felt as if he could see to the very center of my soul. Everything was stripped away, and I felt more vulnerable than I could ever remember.

"What are we doing, Dani?" he asked, his voice husky.

I swallowed thickly, staring at him and feeling the beat of my heart reverberating in every cell of my body. I tried to take a breath, but I couldn't get much air.

"This," I murmured, arching up to catch his lips in another kiss. For a moment, I thought he was going to let it go as his lips molded over mine. But after only one sweep of his tongue, he drew back, his head thumping against the door behind him.

"Dani," he said, his tone low and laced with intensity, "you have no idea how much I want you. But I'm not going to screw everything up worse than it already is by letting this play out like this."

He loosened his hold in my hair, carefully easing me away as he stepped back and straightened. "Just to make it crystal clear," he said bluntly, "I want you. I always have. But we have history, and I don't know what the hell made you so angry with me, but we're going to sort that out before we screw things up even more."

Staring at him, my mouth opened and closed before I snapped it shut. I finally managed to gulp in a breath. All the while, blood rushed through my ears. I was hot, so hot. My nipples were so tight they ached, and I was uncomfortably aware of the throb at the apex of my thighs.

"Wade," I began.

He shook his head. "I can't talk now, Dani. Either I fuck you and make things worse, or I leave. When you're ready to talk, let me know."

At that, he opened the door, a rush of cold air swirling around me as he stepped through and closed the door quickly behind him. I stood there, nearly ready to scream with frustration—a combination of raw need and desire colliding with pure anger. I was furious.

"Fuck you," I muttered, clenching my fist to keep from reaching for the door and chasing after him. I knew it would serve no purpose. Wade could be just as stubborn as I could.

After I managed to get my heart rate under control, I took a lukewarm shower in some sort of effort to cool off and crawled in bed. Unfortunately, I was tense all over and still restless with need.

I found myself reaching between my thighs, sliding my fingers through the slick wetness. Wade was stamped on every reaction of my body. When I tried to push him out of my mind, he crowded my thoughts—the feel of his lips on mine, his hand curving over my bottom, and his name crossing my lips as I brought myself to orgasm moments later.

Chapter Seven

WADE

Striding through the staff kitchen at the lodge, I paused beside the coffee pot. After rinsing my travel mug in the sink, I filled it with coffee and a dash of cream. As I turned, Dani came through the doorway from the back hall where her office was. Her arms were piled high with a massive stack of the white dish towels they went through like crazy in the kitchen.

I was mid-sip when I looked over, my gaze colliding with hers across the room. Even from a good twenty feet away, my body reacted. It felt as if a live wire was suspended in the air between us.

I'd spent the last two nights tossing and turning. I was sleepy and irritable. I was also most definitely wondering why I had to go and be the bigger person in my mind and tell her that we had to talk before I let things go further.

My body had *no* fucking clue what *that* dumb idea was all about. "Mornin', Dani," I called as I lowered my travel mug.

She stopped her brisk stride, a pink flush staining her cheeks. I wanted to walk across the room and tug that elastic free from her ponytail, so I could watch her curls fall around her shoulders before I claimed her mouth again.

For a moment, I thought she wasn't even going to reply to me. Finally, she said, "Mornin', Wade."

At that second, Dawson came through the same door behind her, running into her. Seeing as Dani was standing immediately in front of the doorway, the collision wasn't a surprise.

"Whoa there," he said, catching her by the shoulders when she stumbled slightly.

Her eyes swung to him. "Slow down," she said sharply.

Without another word, she practically ran into the restaurant kitchen up front. Dawson watched her retreat before striding across the room to stop by the coffee pot where I still stood.

He snagged a mug hanging on the shelf above the coffee pot and filled it. "What the hell did you do to piss her off?" he asked casually.

My gaze slid to his. "What the hell makes you think I did anything?"

A grin teased at the corners of Dawson's mouth as he turned and leaned his hips against the counter. "Because you're about the only person who manages to regularly piss Dani off."

I narrowed my eyes and took a welcome sip of the rich, dark brew. I was about to argue the point, but I realized it was futile. With a shrug, I shook my head. "Hell if I know."

Just then, our emergency cell phones simultaneously beeped. Like Jackson and me, Dawson was on the Stolen Hearts Valley Emergency Response Team. I slipped my phone out of my pocket. "Hey, what's up?" I said quickly.

Nick Hudson, the administrative supervisor for our team, replied, "We've got a call out for support to a climbing accident on the north end of the valley. You and Dawson are the first in line for calls today."

"He happens to be standing right beside me. We'll head

out now. I'll call you on the way to get more information," I said before quickly hanging up.

Dawson was already striding across the kitchen. In the back hall, we had a room for equipment. With Jackson one of the team leaders, he made sure we had plenty of equipment on hand here.

"Where we headed?" Dawson asked, all business as we snagged our go-bags.

"Climbing accident toward the north end of the valley. I told Nick we'd call when we're on our way."

We quickly changed before we left and made sure we had enough gear for both of us. I presumed one or both of us would be doing some climbing. With Dawson at the wheel, we sped through the winding roads in the mountains toward our destination. There were several popular hiking and climbing areas in the valley. Nick had already texted us the trail in question, which led to a rock face frequented by climbers since it was easy to access. The puzzling part was why the hell there was an accident at this hour.

"Mind if I put Nick on speaker?" I asked.

"I'd appreciate it if you did."

Sipping my coffee, I pulled my phone out and tapped Nick's number with my thumb. In another moment, he answered. "Just so you know," I explained, "I've got you on speaker. Can you give us the lowdown?"

"Yeah, long story short, two buddies went out for a climb yesterday. The plan was for them to spend the night and climb today and then head out. They were supposed to call and check in, but they never did. I have no idea why the girlfriend waited until this morning to call, but she did. Right after she called because she was concerned, they called. One of the guys fell last night, likely because it's slick this time of year. He thought he was fine, and woke up this morning to his ankle so swollen he can hardly move it. Needless to say, his buddy can't carry him out either. Let me get you the GPS coordinates. Y'all are going to need to hike in about three miles. Also, I just called over to see if Boone and Walker can meet you there."

"Okay, how about you text us those coordinates and let me know if anyone else will meet us there?"

"Will do," Nick replied before ending the call.

Dawson took a long swallow from his travel mug before setting it back in the holder mounted on the dash. "Well, I guess I could use the exercise," he said with a wry grin.

"I'm relieved to find out it's not a major emergency," I said. "I'm sorry for the guy and his ankle, but it sounds like he'll be fine."

Dawson caught my eyes and nodded. Not much later, we arrived at the trailhead with the update from Nick that Boone and Walker would be behind us by a few minutes.

The early morning winter air was bracing. With a light dusting of snow on the ground, we threw our backpacks on, made sure we had our emergency medical kits, and began our hike. It was a beautiful morning with the sky stained lavender and pink as the sun rose slowly over a mountain ridge in the distance.

Birds chattered at us and squirrels announced our arrival as we walked swiftly up the trail toward the climbing area. Dawson glanced over his shoulder at one point, throwing a sly grin my way.

"What?" I asked.

"You never did tell me what you did to piss Dani off this morning."

"Dude, not now," I muttered with a roll of my eyes.

Just then, we heard voices approaching. Looking back, I saw Boone and Walker calling from behind us on the trail. "Damn, they drove fast," I commented.

"Good thing," Dawson added. "We'll need the help, what with carrying a full-grown man for three miles."

They jogged to catch up to us as we continued moving along the trail after a quick wave. Glancing back, I flashed a grin. "Hey, guys. Good to see y'all. Sounds like we'll need some help with transport."

Boone nodded. "That's what I hear from Nick. He had a quick update from them in between his call with you and us. We'll see how it looks when we get there."

Like me, Boone grew up in Stolen Hearts Valley and then moved out West for a few years. Although our paths didn't cross, he led a similar life to mine. He bounced between jobs at various outdoor programs and cut his teeth on the mountain rescue teams out West. With his shaggy dark-blond hair and blue eyes, he had an easygoing, outdoorsy vibe to him.

Dawson greeted Walker, who none of us knew very well yet. "You spent much time on these trails?" Dawson asked.

Walker nodded. "Sure have," he drawled. He fell silent after that.

Considering we were hiking at a swift pace, too much conversation would only slow us down. Walker reminded me a bit of Lucas—tall, dark, and quiet. Although he shared the same black hair, his eyes were a silvery-gray. The moment that thought passed through my mind, I recalled Dani commenting his eyes were like moonlight.

The moment Dani sashayed into my thoughts, she filled every corner of my mind. I was relieved when we arrived at the climbing area within a few minutes. I needed to stay busy. Because I needed Dani *not* to take over every corner of my mind.

Hours later, after we had safely delivered both men to the hospital to be cleared and done a debriefing with Nick, Dawson and I returned to the lodge. I didn't want to say aloud just how much I was hoping to see Dani tonight. I still didn't know why the hell I was trying to be honorable with her.

Without thinking, I found myself striding down the back hallway at the lodge after I had taken a shower in the staff bathroom. I realized if I didn't seek Dani out, she just might box me back into that purgatory we'd been living in together for the last few years. That woman could be so damn stubborn.

When I reached her office door to find it closed, I was just about to knock when I heard her talking. My hand fell slowly, and I listened. Hell, I eavesdropped. I didn't even care if I shouldn't.

"It's complicated," I heard Dani say.

"Everything is complicated," Evie said in reply.

Dani's sigh was audible, even through the door. I smiled to myself because I could practically see her nose wrinkling in frustration. "Evie, just because Wade and I have history doesn't mean we're meant for some kind of happily ever after."

Evie's annoyed sigh also filtered through the door. Convenient for me, these were lightweight hollow doors. "I'm not suggesting you and Wade are destined for happily ever after. I certainly wouldn't suggest that because you guys dated in high school. I'm just saying it's obvious there's chemistry between you two, and has been for as long as I've known you both. You fight it so hard that it's clear the only way you're going to get to the other side of it is to do something about it."

There was a moment of silence, and I could feel the tension emanating through the door.

"Fine, be pissed off at me," Evie said in response to what I could imagine was a frustrated look from Dani. "I'm just telling it like I see it. I mean, you're cranky as hell, so you might as well get some and maybe that will get you to relax a little bit."

Just when I was realizing I shouldn't be lingering in front of the door, it flew open and Evie started to stride out, almost colliding with me.

"Oh," she said, coming to an abrupt stop in front of me. "Perfect. We were just talking about you, Wade."

With that pointed comment, Evie flounced past me. I looked across the room at Dani where she stood beside her desk. Her cheeks were bright red. I tried to think of a way to smooth this over, but quickly decided against it. Dani didn't need to know how much I heard. I certainly didn't mind teasing her with Evie's comment.

"Sounds like Evie thinks you need to get some," I said as I stepped into Dani's office and closed the door behind me.

Dani crossed her arms tightly over her chest, her eyes narrowing to slits as she glared at me and pursed her lips. "You're taking that totally out of context," she said, lifting her chin and looking away from me.

"Pretty sure I'm not," I drawled as I walked closer to her.

Dani's jaw was set in a hard line, tension emanating from her with her shoulders held up stiffly, and her hands balled into fists. Emotion stormed through me. My frustration stemmed from Dani being so fucking stubborn. Just as strong was the frustration I felt with myself.

I knew we somehow needed to get to a point where we could talk about whatever Dani was holding inside. Yet, I also knew this tension between us—a heady mixture of raw lust and desire tinged with the emotion tangled up in our shared past—wasn't going to dissipate from talking.

I took two strides, closing the distance between us. When I came to a stop in front of her, her scent spun around me, once again pushing through the misty curtains of memory and eliciting nothing but pure reaction.

Chapter Eight

WADE

I kicked the gentleman inside of me to the curb. I might be trying to be the bigger one here by insisting we talk, but it was getting us nowhere. Dani wouldn't look at me. I lifted my hand, letting my fingers trail through the ends of her hair. A curly lock bounced free, and I let my thumb trace along the hard line of her jaw.

Dani's eyes finally flicked to mine. I sensed she wanted to look away, but like me, she was too fucking stubborn. There was a tiny kernel of anger still held tight inside me from never quite understanding why she walked away from us.

In that moment, the kernel cracked open, and I wanted to let her have it. But when I saw the vulnerability flickering in her gaze, my heart felt sliced wide open.

That was the thing with us—we had that long, wild tumble into love you can only really experience when you're too young and too stupid to realize just how much love can hurt you. As young and inexperienced as we were, we had a potent chemistry, one that had never really faded. I'd mostly been able to forget about it—or, rather, pretend I had forgotten about it—in the years I lived away from her. But ever since I'd returned to Stolen Hearts Valley, it was a constant battle to ignore it.

All of my other experiences with women paled in comparison to the crazy hot fire that flickered between Dani and me whenever we got too close. My fingertips tingled where I touched her. When I heard the sharp intake of her breath, I took another step closer and completely forgot my stupid goal of insisting we talk before this went any further.

"Dani," I said, my voice husky.

My heart was kicking inside my chest and that familiar, thrumming need raced through every cell, putting my body on high alert.

I swear to God, she meant to argue with me. Probably just for existing.

But when her eyes flashed and she opened her mouth, my name slipped out instead. That was all I needed.

She arched up toward me just as I dipped down toward her. Our lips met, and it was as if lightning struck us from above, its electric force sizzling through my body.

This kiss didn't start slow. There was no teasing, no soft, easy exploration. It was a fucking explosion. Our mouths met in a clash of lips, teeth, and tongue. It was hot, wet, and messy.

My brain fuzzed. The pulse of need that beat between Dani and me took over everything. She was all soft, lush curves with her mouth warm, sweet, and welcoming.

She kissed wildly, her tongue tangling with mine as little frustrated sounds came from the back of her throat. The sound of footsteps coming down the hallway punctured the haze in my mind, and I broke away.

The second I opened my eyes and saw her green eyes dark with need, her lips puffy from our kiss, and her nipples straining against the thin silk of her blouse, it was all I could do not to dive right back in. But this time, I wasn't getting interrupted.

Turning, I strode quickly to the door. I caught myself

just as I was about to slam it shut and carefully closed it, the *click* barely audible. The snick of the lock was a light lash of the whip of lust driving me.

When I turned back to face her, Dani hadn't moved. I held still for several beats. I could hear the rush of blood in my ears with every restless beat of my heart. The sound of Dani's breath coming in soft little pants nearly undid me. With barely a grasp on the reins of my control, I crossed the room. She was still standing immediately in front of her desk. Precisely where I wanted her for what I had in mind.

Dani juggled many roles as the chef and manager of the restaurant. Some nights, she covered as receptionist. I knew tonight was one of those nights because she wore a stretchy skirt. It was cotton and hugged her hips, falling just above her ankles with a little twirl below her knees. She wore a pair of practical leather boots and a loose silk blouse atop her skirt. It was a soft, jade green and matched her eyes.

I leaned my hands on the desk, caging her between my arms. She bit her lip, her breath drawing in slightly.

I let my eyes soak in the sight of her, traveling over the delicate arch of her dark brows, tracing along the sculpted lines of her cheekbones, and idly counting a few of the freckles sprinkled over her nose, almost as a playful afterthought.

Her pink tongue darted out to the corner of her mouth, swiping across her lip just before her teeth dented her plump bottom lip. The need thrumming in my veins tightened, revving like an engine inside of me. If my body was a car, Dani's presence was a heavy foot on the gas pedal.

We'd had each other once before. It might have been years ago. We might have both tried to forget it, to wipe it clean from the shared memory of our bodies. It was all for naught. Getting close to Dani was like a match to dry kindling.

"I've reconsidered," I said with slow deliberation. Despite my effort to gain some control over the fierce lust whipping through my body like a storm, I was barely clinging to my control. My voice was gruff and ragged.

Dani swallowed, her eyes never breaking from mine. I could smell the scent of her arousal and feel my own tighten in my balls, my cock swelling and pressing against my fly.

She cleared her throat before asking, "Reconsidered what?"

"I told you we had to talk first. I've changed my mind."

When my eyes dropped down, I saw her pulse leap at the side of her throat, her skin stained a slight pink over her chest. Her breath came out in a sharp little hiss.

"What do you mean?" she rasped.

"I mean I'm going to make you come so hard, you'll see stars. Make you forget any other man. But don't go thinking you'll get it all."

Her gorgeous green eyes flashed. "How do you know anything is going to happen?" she retorted.

I could sense she was trying to inject her usual bossy tone in her voice. I might not know much, but I knew she was as needy as me in this moment. Her voice came out frayed and husky with need.

Lifting one hand, I gave in to the need to touch her. I cupped a breast, reveling in the feel of her nipple puckering under my thumb. A little sound came from her throat.

"Tell me you don't want to me. Tell me you don't want this. I'll turn around and walk away," I said, lifting my eyes to hers.

The air felt heavy, like the burgeoning before a storm, just before lightning let loose and thunder rumbled through the sky. I waited and when she didn't reply, I added, "I'll walk away, and we'll go back to pretending like there's nothing between us."

She shook her head. Just barely.

"I need words, Dani. Talk to me, and maybe then I'll understand."

Her lips curled with a smile, tugging at my heart. "Don't walk away," she said.

At that, she leaned up and pressed a kiss right at the divot at the base of my throat. That tiny spot, nothing more than her lips touching my skin, was like a brand, the searing heat of it racing through me.

Straightening, I slid my hands down over the curve of her hips, gathering the soft fabric of her skirt in my hands as I inched it up her thighs. When my fingers met the silky soft skin on her thighs, I didn't even bother to hold back my groan.

"Wade," she began, a hint of a question in her tone.

"Just let me do this," I murmured in reply as I lifted her up onto the desk, sliding her hips back and pressing her knees just far enough apart to stand between them.

"Okay," she breathed.

And then, we tumbled back into the fire of another kiss —this one wetter and messier. I fit my mouth over hers and simply gave in. When she wasn't busy thinking, Dani was so fucking responsive, she slayed me.

I needed to taste more of her. That pressing desire was the only thing that could get me to break free of the unholy temptation of her mouth. I dragged my tongue down the soft skin of her neck, satisfaction rolling through me when she whimpered and arched into me. I could feel her tight little nipples pressing against my chest. Her hands got busy, one sliding up my chest and the other gripping my back as I tasted her, tracing along her collarbone and then dipping down into the valley between her breasts.

I tugged on her blouse, shoving it down below her breasts, the loose scoop neck giving me easy access. When I drew back slightly and saw her full breasts pushed together in this ridiculous excuse of a bra, just thin, silky lace, I bit back a groan. Her tight pink nipples teased me through the lace.

"So fucking gorgeous," I murmured, lifting my eyes to

Dani's. Her cheeks flushed pinker, and she looked slightly surprised.

I put that in the parking lot of my brain, wondering how the hell Dani hadn't been worshipped by every man who was graced with the luck of touching her. Leaning down, I closed my mouth over a nipple, straight through the silk, reveling in the sound of her ragged cry as I grazed my teeth over it before giving it a hard suck.

Meanwhile, I pressed her knees further apart and tugged her hips closer to the edge of the desk before cupping my palm over the silk between her thighs. It was soaking wet, the moisture slick on my fingers even through the silk.

Dani murmured something.

I lifted my head. "Yes?" My voice was taut, held in and constrained by the effort it was taking me not to fuck her right here and right now. I might have reconsidered, but I wasn't going to rush this.

Dani shook her head when I met her eyes. Dragging my fingertips over her, I gave myself a little glance down to see her panties matched her cream silk and lace bra. Apparently, Dani had developed a taste for nice lingerie. I honestly couldn't recall what kind of underwear she wore in high school.

I could forgive myself that lapse. I remembered everything important, such as her scent, the feel of her, and the thrumming passion between us. I could forgive my seventeen-year-old, horny self the oversight of not remembering what kind of underwear Dani had been wearing when we lost our virginity to each other.

When I looked up again, Dani shrugged. "I think I said please," she finally mumbled.

Somehow, it was endearing for her to answer honestly. I slipped a finger over that soaking wet silk, pushed it to the side, and trailed my fingers through her slick, swollen folds. "Damn, Dani, I might think you want me as much as I want you," I murmured as I leaned down to suck her other nipple in my mouth right as I let a finger sink inside her core.

She gasped, her hips bucking into my hand. "Oh God, Wade," she cried out when I nipped lightly on her nipple and added another finger to the first, driving them in knuckle deep and savoring the way her channel clenched and rippled around my touch.

I sensed she was already on the edge. As much as I remembered how it felt to be with Dani, it had been years ago, and we'd been young. I didn't have the map of her body and her responses memorized the way I wished I did. But, I'd had enough experience since then to sense the quickening, to feel the rock of her hips into my fingers.

I needed to taste her before this was over and bent low to drop hot, damp kisses along her collarbone.

Chapter Nine

DANI

"I need to taste you," Wade growled against my skin.

I was already building toward climax, everything in my body hanging on the precipice, with pleasure spinning in wild eddies. The ache at my core was almost unbearable.

"Wade!" I cried, almost in dismay when he drew his fingers out from between my thighs.

I was beyond shame, beyond caring I had allowed myself to give in to this. All I knew was what I needed, and I needed it now. "Don't you dare stop," I ordered as I felt his hand press on my thigh, my own juices trailing over my skin as his hand moved down slightly.

Wade's eyes were dark when he looked up at me, a grin kicking up one corner of his mouth. "Oh, I won't stop, darlin'. I just need you to come on my tongue."

His blunt words sent a blast of heat through me. Then, he was pushing my thighs further apart and leaning forward to bring his mouth against me.

Oh. My. God. This was a decadent, delicious torture I had never experienced.

Wade licked into my core, swirling his tongue around my

clit and then stretching my pussy open with his fingers again. It had been a while, such a while that I was tight and the feel of him stretching me open was so intense, I could hardly take it. My fingers threaded into his hair and I held on as he fucked me with his mouth and fingers. I had no sense of time, but my orgasm was abrupt and overpowering. It hit me so hard I heard the rough shout of his name, the pleasure acute. It spun tight and then snapped loose again, splitting me wide open as it wracked my body with bone-deep shudders.

I barely recognized myself as I slowly came to. I was limp, and the only thing holding me up was Wade as he slid a hand around my back, steadying me as I started to fall back on the desk.

I almost cried out again when he slowly straightened. Unabashed, he reached for a tissue from the box on my desk and wiped it over his mouth, only after sliding his tongue lazily across his lips, his eyes on mine the entire time.

———

The following evening, I strode through the restaurant, menus in hand as I led another group to a large table in the corner. As I set the menus down and rounded the table to fill waters, my eyes were snagged by motion just to the side of the view through the windows out front.

Even from a distance, where the two men walking together certainly weren't visible beyond a distant outline, I knew the man on the right was Wade. He walked with an easy strength and confidence. I wouldn't quite call it swagger because that would imply arrogance. The chasm between arrogance and the type of assurance Wade had was significant.

Wade's confidence was elemental. He had nothing to prove. It was all raw strength. And so fucking sexy, it took my breath away.

A flush suffused my entire body at nothing more than the distant sight of him. Given the time of day, I presumed he was just finishing up from the construction he, Lucas, and a few of the other guys had been working on with the addition of more guest cabins over in that area.

My mind flashed to the look in his eyes last night after he had brought me to the most intense climax of my life. It was fair to say our previous heated kisses in high school and our single sexual encounter beyond kisses had come a long way.

I was so distracted that I gave a start when a customer repeated my name. Swinging my head away from the windows, I looked over at the friendly elderly woman smiling at me. "Dani Love, right?"

"Yes," I replied.

The woman nodded. "So good to see you," she said. She was definitely familiar, but I couldn't place why.

"Can I go ahead and take your drink order?" I asked, pulling out the small computer tablets we used for ordering. "Your waitress will be here shortly to go over specials and the like, but I can certainly get you started with drinks if you know what you'd like."

"That would be great," a man in the group replied. "You carry the Lost Deer brewery line, correct?"

"We sure do. What can I get for you?"

I quickly entered their orders and hurried off to deal with the next group of customers waiting up front. I was relieved for how busy my job was. I didn't need time to dwell on what I had allowed to happen last night in my office. I'd lost my freaking mind.

Even worse, Wade filled every corner of it. Whenever there was a moment to breathe, any time where I wasn't entirely focused, my thoughts squirreled around him. My body, my traitorous body, kept replaying our encounter. The reverberations of how it felt to be with him again were visceral.

Here and there, as I hurried around the restaurant helping bus tables, checking in with the wait staff in the kitchen, and cycling new groups of customers to the tables in an endless rotation, my eyes kept traveling to that woman who appeared to know who I was. That, in itself, wasn't out of the ordinary. Stolen Hearts Valley was a sprawling area in the Blue Ridge Mountains, but most of the long-term residents usually knew of each other, even if only in passing.

But with that woman, something kept nudging the back of my mind. It was slightly uncomfortable. Not her, per se, but however I knew her.

I happened to be crossing the guest parking lot out back at one point later in the evening. The kitchen was hopping so quickly, I'd snagged the overflowing garbage near the dishwashing station to take it out myself. Little things like that were what I did all day when we had busy times out front. Our dishwasher needed to focus on moving those dishes through and not worry about dealing with the trash.

Not to mention, I needed the fresh air. I was hot. Nights like tonight kept me on my feet and moving. Whenever I told myself I could use a little trim down and that I should sign up for a gym, I had a night like tonight and remembered running a restaurant was one hell of a workout.

The woman who seemed to know me happened to be standing by her car as one of the couples in their party was saying good night. "Night, Mom," a younger woman said. She gave a little wave before walking across the parking lot to climb into a car.

I lifted the lid to the dumpster and tossed the bag in, savoring the chilly air chasing over my skin. Christmas was only three and a half weeks away now. Although it wasn't technically winter yet, it was cold and my breath misted in the air. I wondered if we'd have a white Christmas this year. The Southern mountains certainly got snow, but it wasn't like up North, or out West. We had snow and icy, winding roads, but we were never guaranteed a white Christmas. I loved the snow in the wintertime here. It was such a contrast to the languid, hot summers.

I smiled politely at the woman as I passed by her car. She was pulling out her keys and paused, turning toward me. "You don't recognize me, do you?" she asked.

Stopping at the back of her car, I shook my head. "I don't. I'm sorry. You do seem familiar, but I can't quite place you. Care to refresh my memory?"

She was quiet for a few beats, her gaze thoughtful. "Well, it might be an awkward subject, but I was the head nurse on duty when you came to the hospital when you were in high school."

In a blinding second, my memory sharpened. I remembered her warm brown gaze. She was the nicest person there, at least to me, and had been there for me during several hours where I felt more alone than I ever had in my life.

Swallowing, I nodded slowly. "Oh, now I recognize you."

Her return smile held a tinge of sadness. "Every so often, I wonder how people I've seen in the hospital are doing. I never forgot you. I'm glad to see you're doing okay."

Life could be strange, so very strange. This woman, who had been present for nothing more than a few hours of my life, had seen me stripped to my emotional bones. She took a few steps. "You take care, dear."

I felt numb, my fingers tingling and my head buzzing. "I will," I managed. "Have a good night." Manners shaped my words by force of pure habit.

I stood there as she climbed in her car, the sound of the door closing with a *click* finally galvanizing me. The engine to her car rumbled to life just as I looked up to see Wade standing a few cars away. His eyes were dark, and his gaze inscrutable. I had no idea what he was thinking, but I knew he'd just heard that interaction.

A sense of panic clawed at me.

"Dani!" The sound of my name broke through the panic,

tightening like a vise around me. Snapping my head to the side, I saw Evie leaning out the door from the back kitchen.

Without a word to Wade, I turned and strode across the parking lot. "Sorry," I said, as I reached Evie still waiting at the door. "I got sidetracked by a customer."

Evie looked past me. "Wade is a customer?" she teased.

Flustered, I shook my head as I looked back at him. "No, that woman," I said, pointing to the car now backing up.

"Got it," Evie replied, looking doubtful. Given the look on Wade's face—I still wasn't quite sure how to interpret it —I sensed Evie didn't believe me.

We didn't have time for this. "Anyway," I said, stepping past her, "what's up?"

"Oh, a little dispute up front over reservations. We need your touch to resolve this one."

On most long days, I didn't leap at the chance to deal with annoyed customers. Oh, I managed them with a deft touch, but it wasn't my preferred part of this job. Tonight, however, I would gladly step in and mediate a dispute over reservations. That was a million times easier than even thinking about the nurse from the hospital and what Wade overheard.

Chapter Ten

WADE

I shouldered through the door into the offices for the vet clinic. I was beyond frustrated today. When Jackson had called over and said he had forgotten a box of emergency supplies for the vet clinic, I had happily volunteered to drive them over.

Lucas was standing in the hallway, his daughter Rylie leaning against his hip as he idly stroked his fingers through her hair while he talked to Shay. "Well, you can count me among the people that are relieved that stallion is gone," he said.

"What's a stallion, Daddy?" Rylie asked, looking up at Lucas.

Lucas smiled down to her. "It's a man horse," he explained.

"Mischief's a boy, and you like him," Rylie returned, referring to a rescue horse beloved on the farm and well-known for his antics. Mischief was prone to jumping out of the pasture, but he was a friendly guy so he caused little fuss.

Shay was grinning at this exchange when she looked up

to see me coming down the hall with two boxes in my arms. "Have fun figuring out how to explain that," she said to Lucas with a soft laugh.

"Better yet, you can help me with these boxes," I offered.

Lucas looked downright relieved. "Mind if I steal your dad?" I asked, glancing to Rylie, who had stepped away from her father's side and was presently looking up at me.

Her dark curls bounced when she shook her head. "I'll help too," she announced.

"Sweet pea, those boxes are almost as heavy as you," Lucas said with a smile. "How about you be in charge of the door?"

"I can do that," Rylie chirped.

"Thank you, Wade," Shay said as she reached me.

"Jackson tied up?" I asked.

"Yes, emergency surgery. A dog got hit by a car." Shay's lips twisted with a sigh. "He's already in there doing surgery, but that's when he realized we had a new order of surgery supplies. When the delivery guy came, he left them over at the lodge instead of bringing them to the clinic," she explained as she hurried ahead of me to open the door into the supply room here. I set the boxes down while Shay stayed behind to sort through and organize them on the shelves.

Rylie was already stationed by the door when I approached. She promptly opened the door, using both hands to turn the stainless-steel knob.

"Thank you, Rylie," I drawled as I passed by.

"You're welcome, Wade!"

I might've still been stewing over that mysterious snippet of conversation I heard in the parking lot last night between Dani and a customer, but I could use the distraction of Rylie's innocent cheer.

Lucas's daughter was around more often since he and Valentina had gotten together. Lucas frequently stopped by to pick up Valentina at the clinic where her office was. She handled all of the accounting and bookkeeping for the lodge, the rescue program, and Jackson's vet clinic. She also picked up shifts at the restaurant when needed.

Rylie's mother had passed away before Lucas and Valentina got together. While his life was mostly work and being a father, now that he had a reason to hang around, we saw him more often, and by extension, Rylie.

When I returned to the parking lot, Lucas was standing at the back of my truck. "Everything in here?" he asked as he reached for a box.

"All of it. You can handle it, man. You're strong," I teased.

Lucas chuckled. "Right."

"Well, Jackson's got the hard job since he's doing emergency surgery. I figure I can handle the grunt work."

"True," Lucas replied. With Rylie doing the honors at the door several more times, he and I had everything unloaded within a few minutes.

"Are you here to pick up Valentina?" I asked as we paused in the hallway.

"Uh-huh," Rylie announced, answering for him as she spun in a circle, stopping in front of us.

Lucas smiled down at her. Looking back to me, he added, "I thought Valentina was here, but she's over at the restaurant. She said one of the waitresses called out with a cold."

Glancing at the clock mounted above the door at the end of the hallway, I commented, "Well, it's certainly busy tonight over there."

"So I hear. That's why we're gonna head home so you don't miss your bedtime." Lucas glanced down at Rylie.

"How will Valentina get home?" she chirped.

"Shay said she'd give her a ride." Looking back to me, Lucas explained, "Valentina's car is in the shop. I've been telling her I knew there was something up with the brakes, and she finally took it in. I wish she'd get a new one, but she's not going for it yet." At that, he reached for Rylie's hand. "We need to go. It's only a half an hour until your bedtime."

I waved good night to them, then found myself standing alone in the hallway. With nothing to do, my mind immediately spun back to wondering why the hell I didn't know Dani had been in the hospital in high school.

What for? My thoughts turned that question over and over, getting nowhere since I had no clues to guide me. I didn't know why, but I sensed it had something to do with the way she broke things off with me.

I knew it would be hours before I could get some time alone with her, but I intended to talk to her tonight.

———

Hours later, after heading out to Lost Deer Bar to grab a drink and pass the time with a game of pool because I was too fucking restless to stay at home, I parked in the staff parking lot behind the lodge restaurant. As I walked past the kitchen entrance, I heard the distinct sound of Gloria, the massive pig who had the run of the farm and was beloved by the staff and guests. Pausing, I glanced in the direction of the sound to see Gloria making her way toward me, her feet shuffling through the frosty leaves.

"Hey girl," I called, pausing because no matter how anxious I was to find Dani, it just wouldn't do to ignore Gloria.

Gloria ended up at the rescue program Jackson ran after she turned out *not* to be a mini pig. She was anything but mini as pigs went. She reached me, nudging my knee with her nose as I leaned down to scratch between her ears. "Shouldn't you be in your stall?" I asked conversationally.

"Yes, she should." Shay's voice reached me as she

rounded the corner of the building. "I obviously didn't latch the barn door after the evening feeding." She stopped beside us, glancing down to Gloria and commenting affectionately, "It's too cold for you to be out and about. I bet you thought you might come get some dinner scraps."

Gloria lifted her head and eyed Shay before stepping closer to her and pressing her round body against her hip. Shay glanced at me. "I'll walk her back to the rescue barn. See you tomorrow."

"'Night," I replied, watching as they began walking toward the path that led toward where the clinic and rescue barns were.

After another moment, I strode through the trees, my gaze scanning until it landed on Dani's cabin. When I saw the lights on, the tension bundled tight in my chest eased slightly.

Stepping onto the small porch, I lifted my fist, hesitating slightly. Not giving myself a chance to debate the wisdom of this, I let my knuckles fall sharply on the door. After a moment, I heard footsteps, and Dani swung the door open. She'd changed out of her work outfit and wore a faded cotton sweatshirt and leggings that hugged her curvy hips, with bright blue socks. She looked so gorgeous, I lost my breath for a moment. Her face was rosy as if she'd just washed it, my eyes narrowing in on the freckles dancing over her nose.

Fuck me. All I had to do was look at her and I wanted her.

Swallowing, I asked, "Can I come in?"

Her eyes searched my face for a few seconds before she nodded. "Sure."

Stepping back, she opened the door wider to let me pass. A gust of cool air blew in as Dani moved to close the door behind me. The silence came abruptly when the door clicked shut.

Turning, I found Dani with her arms crossed tightly in front of her chest. Her thumb and forefinger were rubbing the faded cuff of her sleeve. I suspected she knew I had overheard the end of her conversation in the parking lot. Lifting my eyes, I saw the resolute set of her jaw and the tension at the corners of her eyes.

One of the things I had always loved about Dani was she didn't hide much. She was pretty open book with her emotions practically written in bold magic marker on her face. The downside to that was when she was trying to hide something, it was more obvious.

She walked past me toward the small kitchenette in the corner. "Do you want some hot cocoa?"

Somehow, her question seemed entirely out of place. A chuckle rumbled in my chest. Looking over her shoulder, she shrugged. "It's cold out," she said, her voice a little frayed on the edges.

Following her over, I sank down into one of the chairs at the small round table when she gestured toward it. "Sure. Never any good reason to turn down cocoa, right?"

"Especially not if I'm adding some marshmallow vodka."

"Damn. Never had that, but it sounds good."

I watched as she puttered around, filling a tea kettle, heating milk, and getting out actual chocolate to melt into the milk. This was Dani. Of course, she didn't do the powdered type of hot cocoa.

After a few minutes, she sat down across from me, her knees bumping into mine before she drew them back quickly. Her eyes met mine across the table. Before I had a chance to ask, the truth flew out of her mouth and slammed into me. "I got pregnant. And if you remember, I was away that summer after we ..." She paused, circling her hand. I didn't need her to explain that she was referring to the one and only time we had sex, so I simply nodded as shock reverberated through me. "My dad freaked out and told me I couldn't see you again. It turns out I had an ectopic preg-nancy and had a miscarriage. I almost bled to death."

My breath simply left my lungs. I felt as if a boulder slammed into me. My chest ached, and I felt physically sick. Just as I reached for her hands—because I needed to touch her—the kettle whistled right behind us.

Dani practically jumped out of her chair, spinning around to turn off the propane burner. I barely registered what she was doing. In the few moments it took for her to add some water to the milk and chocolate mixture, I tried to gather myself together. She sat back down across from me. The room was so quiet, the sound of the marshmallow vodka as she poured it into the mugs was loud.

When she handed me a mug, I wrapped my hands around it as if it were a rope and I was drowning at sea. I felt tossed asunder, caught in a riptide of emotion I didn't even quite understand.

I finally rasped, "What?"

Dani stirred her cocoa, the sound of the spoon clinking around the edges sharp. After a moment, she replied, "That kind of came out really fast. I'm sorry."

"Jesus, Dani. You don't need to be sorry for anything. I'm sorry. I had no idea."

"I know," she said softly. "I wanted to tell you, but it was all kinds of crazy."

"So, you're telling me we had sex once, and you had the bad luck to get pregnant and then have a miscarriage and almost die?"

She swallowed, sadness entering her gaze before she stirred her cocoa again. She took a sip before lowering her mug slowly. "That woman, the one who was talking to me in the parking lot?" At my nod, she continued, "She was one of the nurses on duty that night. She told me it's really easy to get pregnant when you're seventeen. She said you can even get pregnant through your clothes when you're that young." Dani's smile was sad, and I sensed she was trying to find humor in an experience that had none.

Her shoulders rose and fell when she took a breath before lifting her mug to take a sip. "I'll say it a little slower this time. We had sex. One time. I got pregnant. If you recall, I was gone the whole summer because we were out visiting my dad's parents at their place in Colorado. I don't know if you remember, but at first, I texted and I even sent you that card."

Her lips curled in an actual smile then, and my heart felt bruised. Because I'd tried not to remember. I kind of shoved it out of my mind, but just now, I knew exactly where that card was. It was tucked in a box of things from my bedroom when I was a kid in a closet somewhere at my parents' house. While I was absorbing this shocking truth, my emotions felt battered as everything else I'd tried to shove away rose from the mists of my memory like visceral blows.

"I found out early that I was pregnant because I had morning sickness pretty bad. My mom figured it out. She promised she wouldn't tell my dad, but he overheard us talking about it after she went and got me a pregnancy test. He was furious." Dani sighed, lifting a hand and winding one of her curls around her fingers. She wasn't often nervous, so when she was, it nearly broke my heart. "So, there you go. That's why I stopped talking to you. I didn't want him to freak out on you."

I stared at Dani, unsettled, disoriented, and almost afraid. More than anything, it killed me to grasp how she must have felt. I took a gulp of the hot cocoa, distantly noticing the marshmallow flavor and savoring the burn of the vodka.

This time, when I reached for her hand, she didn't pull away. It was clammy and cold in mine. When I brushed my thumb across her wrist, I could feel the shallow, rapid beat of her pulse.

"When you had a miscarriage, was that when you were at your grandparents' place?"

Dani shook her head quickly, her curls swinging around her shoulders as she did. "No. It was right after we got back."

"I'm so fucking sorry, Dani," I finally said, my voice thick from the emotion clotted in my throat.

"You don't have anything to apologize for, Wade. I shut you out. I never even told you what really happened. I just threw a slushy at you when you tried to talk to me at school that fall." Her smile was bitter. It faded quickly, and she bit her lip as she looked at me across the table. "I'd like to say I would have even if you hadn't heard what must've been a confusing bit in the parking lot there. But I don't know. It just seemed easier to not say anything."

I felt compelled to explain. "Just so you know, I wasn't trying to eavesdrop the other night. All I heard when I was walking to my truck was something about you being in the hospital in high school. Needless to say, I was confused."

"I can imagine."

I finally took another sip of my hot cocoa. It slid down my throat smoothly. "I'd give your dad hell if he was still alive for me to do so," I said as I gave her hand a squeeze.

Dani lifted a shoulder in a tiny shrug. "It's all water under the bridge now. I think he just kind of freaked out. I'm not a father, so it's hard for me to know what it might be like to find out that my seventeen-year-old daughter was pregnant. While he was furious and forbade me from talking to you, he was basically no help whatsoever. My mom was supportive. She told me I could do whatever I wanted and she would support my decision. She's a nurse, so she said she'd seen more than her share of young mothers feeling like they had no choice. He did say he wouldn't stand in the way of an abortion if I got one, but the choice was taken out of my hands."

"What did you want to do?" I asked. Manufactured from whole cloth, my mind conjured an image of Dani pregnant and our imaginary child with her dark curls and freckled cheeks.

"I didn't know what I wanted. I was so freaked out, Wade. I don't know what would've happened if I hadn't been away all summer when I found out. It all blew up in such a weird fucked-up way, and I didn't know what to do. I was throwing up all the time, and then I was bleeding everywhere one afternoon and the decision was made for me. Before I even realized what was happening, my mother was with me at the hospital bossing all the ER staff around. She was pissed they wouldn't let her handle anything, but it was a conflict because I'm her daughter. Since she's a nurse, she knew how serious it was."

My throat nearly closed up and my eyes stung. I could hardly bear the thought that Dani had to make her way through all of that mostly alone.

"Did anybody other than your parents know?"

"The staff at the hospital, but that's it. It's pretty heavy, not exactly the kind of thing to vent about with my friends, you know? Maybe if I'd been home over the summer, I probably would've talked to some of my friends, but it was also kind of embarrassing."

Emotion was spinning like a tornado inside of me, a mix of anger at Dani's now-deceased father, at the world, at bad luck, and a stinging pain that she waited this long to tell me. Despite that pain, I understood why. She'd only been seventeen. Her father had always been strict, and I couldn't even fathom how he handled this.

Life could be so strange. Ever since Dani had basically cut me out, I'd been confused until I decided it wasn't worth it. She'd been so easy to be with. We'd been friends first and danced around dating before we actually did. There was always a push and pull with her because she was a bit prickly and feisty and that was her nature. We traveled into a few months of pushing the envelope further and further, with stolen kisses when we were alone and then that one night. One night that took her innocence in so many layers. I fancied myself in love with her before she went away that summer.

With blinding clarity, I realized I still loved her although I'd barely let myself consider it. I loved her in that soul deep way it's so hard for so many people to find. Yet, we had this tangled mess between us, and I had no idea how she really felt. Oh, I knew we had chemistry, but chemistry was just that.

"Are you okay?" My question came out gruff, the ragged edges of my pain showing.

Dani looked startled, a little laugh escaping. "Of course I'm okay. I'm right here. It's been years. See?" she said, gesturing her hand up and down her body before pausing to take a gulp of her hot cocoa.

"I didn't mean physically."

Her eyes searched mine. "It sucked. I won't lie. I'm relieved, you know. Maybe now you understand why I was a little tense."

"Tense? Is that what you were?"

"I don't know how else to describe it. I felt like shit because I didn't want it to be a thing with my dad with you, so I just never told you what happened. And I hate it. I mean, it's not like we were engaged, or we'd even been together all that long. But we'd been friends first, and it just felt shitty. I felt guilty about not telling you. It was scary and weird. I don't know if I would've gotten through it if it hadn't been for my mom."

I gulped my hot cocoa again, needing the burn of alcohol in the moment.

"Need some more?" she asked when I set the mug down.

"I'd love some more. That marshmallow vodka is about perfect with it."

If I could focus on the surface, maybe I wouldn't lose my mind.

Dani grinned as she stood, fetching my mug as she drained hers. She seemed to need something mundane to do as much as I needed the simple actions of acting like everything was normal to get me through this. I waited at the table, almost stunned into silence. The soft sounds of her pouring cocoa into the mugs and the spoon clinking the edges as she stirred in the vodka were somehow soothing.

After she sat back down and we both had a few more sips of the even stronger cocoa, Dani asked, "Can we not talk about this all night?"

Relief pierced me, because I was out of words and didn't know what else to say. I chuckled, reaching over and squeezing her hand. "Deal. I guess it was pretty heavy."

"Ya think?" she teased, her gaze sobering quickly. "I finally tell you my big bad secret on why I cut you out like that. Yeah, it's heavy. Something else I've had to get used to is, there's nothing I can do to fix it. I can't undo it. I've always hated that. I want a do-over, and that's not an option."

"Dani, you were seventeen. I think you probably did the best you could in a really shitty situation. You meant a lot to me, and it fucking sucked and I was confused. Now, I get it. But I sure as hell don't blame you. I'm just as upset that I wasn't there for you."

She twisted her mouth to the side. "You couldn't be. You didn't know. And we're still talking about it, although I guess I kept it going," she said, before taking a gulp of her cocoa.

"I missed you." My words slipped out. I hadn't even known I was going to say them. But they were so fucking true it was as if they had to be said, the words themselves insisting upon it.

Dani's eyes widened, and I felt that sense of defensiveness I knew so well from her start to rise. But then, she gave her head a little shake and straightened her shoulders. "I'm right here," she teased.

"That's all I get?" I couldn't help but push, just a little bit.

A flush stained her cheeks and her breath came out in a little huff. "I missed you too, Wade."

That meant more than she could ever know.

"I hate drama," she said next.

"Is this drama?"

She rolled her eyes. "It feels like it. The saving grace in that whole fiasco was that hardly anyone knew what happened. Aside from my parents, the only people who knew where those who treated me at the ER that night. And they weren't allowed to gossip."

"I'd give anything for you not to have gone through that alone."

"I know you would've," she said softly.

"There's one thing we can have a do-over on," I added.

"What's that?"

"Us."

Dani's eyes widened. "What do you mean?"

"Exactly that. You know there's a reason we just can't get this chemistry to quit. We might as well see where it goes."

Now, her eyes were wide as saucers, and I wondered if I had overplayed my hand. If there was one thing this last half an hour or so represented, it was brutal honesty. I didn't know what was going to happen, but I knew I wanted a shot, the shot we never got before.

She nibbled on her bottom lip, catching a curl in her fingers and twirling it. "I don't know, Wade."

"Is there someone else?" I finally asked the question that had been practically burning a hole inside my brain.

She shook her head swiftly. "Oh God, no. I mean, the other night wouldn't have ever happened. You know that."

"I figured, but what do we have to lose?"

Chapter Twelve

DANI

Wade nearly leveled me with that question. My heart was thudding wildly in my chest with anxiety spinning in nervous flutters in my belly. You see, there were so many things I told myself I couldn't have.

I'd never been good at relaxing, especially not with men. What happened with Wade, although it was in no way his responsibility, had fucked me up in the head. I was tense about sex. And yes, we used a condom. Turns out, they were right in sex ed—no birth control was one hundred percent.

I tried dating a few times, and it had never gone well. I was too tense, even more tense than usual. After that pregnancy and almost deadly miscarriage, I had a whole list of things to worry about if I were to get pregnant again. One thing I knew about Wade was he had always wanted kids. You'd think most high school boys wouldn't talk about that, but he did.

What if I couldn't give him something I knew he deeply wanted?

With Wade's gaze on me like a laser, my mouth opened, then closed, and then opened again. Wade's big hand curled over mine again. I hadn't even noticed I was cold. I was so rattled. That pesky arousal that always seemed to flare whenever he was near kept me hot and bothered inside. Meanwhile, this entire conversation was so unsettling that I was running hot and cold.

His thumb brushed back and forth over the sensitive skin on the inside of my wrist. My eyes fell, almost shocked at the sight. This man who had once been a boy I believed I loved was now holding my hand.

Wade was a bear of a man. He easily cleared six feet and then some, with broad shoulders. The rest of him was all brawn and muscle, all the way to his hands. He had strong, rugged hands. The calloused surface of his palm holding mine sent little sparks skittering across the surface of my skin.

"There's always something to lose," I finally replied, my voice thick with emotion.

Wade's thumb stilled, and I felt trapped in the intensity of his gaze. "Of course there's always something to lose," he replied slowly.

Like a sharp piece of gravel striking a windshield, with the sound enough to make you jump, I remembered Wade's mother died when he was a little boy. When his dad remarried, his stepmother adopted him. She was lovely and wonderful and everything a boy could want in a mother. Yet, he'd still lost his first mother. I suddenly felt small, not thinking about just how thoroughly he knew that lesson.

"Wade ..." I began, quieting when he shook his head quickly.

"No need to go there, Dani. It's just, I understand. I can't say I know what it was like for you, but I know there's always something to lose. I happen to think we lose the most by not even trying."

We sat there at that small table, simply staring at each other. With every second that passed, my heart knocked wildly inside my chest and flutters spun in my belly as heat suffused me. Wade's dark chocolate gaze chased away the chill lingering from my emotional dump. It had been *so* hard to carry that secret. I hadn't realized just how heavy it had been until now when I had finally let it be known. Sometimes secrets chipped away at your heart.

Are you really going to try to tell him now?

My go-to coping skills to deal with what had transpired between Wade and me had been avoidance and denial. They went hand-in-hand. My avoidance was just not letting myself get too close to him. I never denied the pain of what happened. What I denied was letting myself think Wade could ever have meant more to me.

When Wade's thumb brushed, just once, over my wrist, it sent a streak of fire chasing across my skin and spinning into the heat suffusing every fiber of my body.

I stood from the table abruptly, almost snatching my hand from his. Hugging my arms around my waist, I realized I was almost shaking. My go-to coping skills were failing, because if I couldn't avoid him right now, then my denial couldn't kick in and protect me.

I was fighting a war inside myself. Wanting to snap at him and tell him to fucking leave, and wanting to fling myself into his arms and ask him to make me forget everything.

But that way lay the abyss of uncertainty. I was so afraid to let myself really want him. Rising through the cacophony inside was my heart, beating fast and true. No matter what, I wanted Wade.

Wade, with his long freaking arms, reached out and caught the hem of my shirt, tugging me close. "Okay, stop thinking so hard. Look, I didn't mean to push, or to rush you."

He stopped when I shook my head. "You're not pushing."

His lips curled, just the slightest bit, at the corners. The warmth in his eyes nearly undid me, because that was what made me fall so hard for Wade before. Somehow, his presence was soothing to me. Or it had been, once upon a time. The last few years, I'd been so busy avoiding him, and trying *really* hard to forget that.

I bit my lip, worrying it with my teeth. I tried to take a deep breath, but my pulse was a little too wild for that. "You're not rushing me," I finally said. "It's just ..."

When I couldn't get the words out, Wade tugged me a little closer, reaching for one of my hands. I took a breath as his warmth closed around my cold hand again. "You always were a worrier. I would imagine now you worry more than you used to."

"Why do you say that?" I asked, my voice frayed. I hated the sense of vulnerability I felt when I didn't have my guard up around him. But there wasn't much to do about it.

"Well, lots of people worry about getting pregnant. Hell, we even used a condom. Didn't much matter. It sounds like you went through hell."

I suddenly didn't want to dwell on this anymore. If denial wasn't going to do its job anymore, I would just give in to the current of desire racing through me and sweeping me out to sea.

There was only one person who could keep it from sucking me under. And right now, his warm, dark gaze held mine.

"Can we stop talking?" I asked.

Uncertainty flickered in his eyes, but he didn't back away. Wade wasn't that kind of man. Oh no. He pulled me a little closer until I was standing between his knees. Blood rushed in my ears as my heartbeat galloped along madly.

Uncurling his hand from the hem of my shirt, his hands slid to the dip of my waist to rest on the other side. "Is this when you tell me to get the hell out of here?"

Hope shot up a flare in my heart, its brightness almost blinding in the darkness of the tiny corner where I'd shut it away.

I swallowed and shook my head. "No."

Because I didn't know what else to do, and I was all out of words, I lifted my hand, trailing my thumb over the scruff along his jaw. I traced up around his lips right before I leaned forward and pressed my lips to his. With him seated and me standing between his knees, our faces were almost exactly level. I could feel energy coming off of him in waves and the sense of restraint as he held himself back.

My heart, which I had armored behind steel doors and special locks, broke free. It felt achy and sore and naked, as if I had shielded it from the very sun for too long and now it might burn from the heat of it.

I needed Wade not to hold back. Because if he did, then I might start to think. And thinking never took me anywhere good. At least not when it came to Wade.

Drawing back just a tiny bit, I spoke. "Don't you hold back on me, Wade." My lips brushed against his with every word. The sensation was subtle, but each word sent streaks of heat spiraling through me where they spun into the fire building at my core.

"Bossy much?" he murmured.

The feel of his lips curving in a smile against mine sent my heart into a whirl. I giggled.

"That's my girl," he murmured, this time my heart clenching so tightly it almost hurt.

Thank God I didn't get a chance to think. Wade angled his head to the side, sliding one of his palms up my spine to tangle in my hair as he fit his mouth over mine and kissed me.

Our kiss got hot real fast. With his tongue gliding against mine and the low sound of approval that came from the back of his throat, I was a needy girl in a matter of seconds. Stepping closer, I sighed into his mouth at the feel of his hard, muscled chest pressing against me.

Restless, I made an impatient sound in my throat. He tore his lips free from mine on a groan. "Fuck, darlin', you're going to drive me crazy."

"That's what I was going for," I said breathlessly.

In a distant corner of my mind, I marveled at myself. This girl—one who giggled, one who got breathless—was a girl I thought was long gone.

That same tiny corner of my mind was a little worried, a little worried I might fall too hard. I never had been able to sort out the tangle of how I really felt after the way things went sideways with Wade. It all got so messy, and I was a jumble of emotion, inside and out.

But when I looked into his eyes and saw nothing but desire, my thighs clenched, and I felt lucky. With every beat of my heart drumming that I should let go, this felt *so* right. I actually believed I shouldn't worry about anything but this very moment.

"We're not doing this in a chair," Wade said gruffly as he loosened his hand in my hair and set me back away from him slightly.

"You got a problem with chairs?" I teased as I stepped back when he stood.

A hot shiver skated over my skin when he rose to his full height. Back before I clung to denial and avoidance, I'd always loved how much of a man Wade was. Even in high school, before he filled out completely, he exuded this easy sense of masculinity. It wasn't something he strived to be. He simply was. Tall, strong, bordering on brawny, but with that easy smile and that generous spirit.

He leaned down, his eyes hot on mine. "I have nothing against chairs, and we'll have to give one a spin. But not tonight." With that heated promise, he pressed hot open-mouthed kisses along the side of my jaw. Little fires lit under my skin everywhere his lips landed.

I'd had a few flings since Wade. Or rather, I should say I *tried* to have a few flings. I hadn't consummated the act with anyone since Wade and the disastrous consequences that came from our single time. Part of me thought I was all fucked up about sex. It was just that, even though Wade and I had been young, the chemistry came so easy.

In the few times when things got further along, I never felt like this—not even close. With Wade, even his kisses melted me from the inside out. I was literally like melted butter in his hands.

As his kisses made their way down the side of my neck, one of his hands slid up under my sweatshirt. The feel of his palm coasting over my skin elicited a low cry from my throat.

"Ah, Dani," he groaned, "you're killing me." The backs of his fingers teased under the curves of my breasts.

I hadn't been expecting company so I wasn't wearing a bra. I was in my comfy, baggy clothes, which weren't the least bit sexy. Not at all. It said something about what Wade did to me that I felt sexy as hell the second his eyes lit with the fire I knew was reflected in mine.

He lightly cupped a breast, his hands warm and the feel of his thumb brushing over my nipple bringing it to a tight peak. I gripped his hair when he pressed another hot kiss at that soft spot where my shoulder met my neck.

I didn't realize I had said his name until he lifted his head, his eyes searing into mine. "Yeah?"

I felt my cheeks flush, but I was already so hot inside and out, I didn't suppose it mattered.

"Just don't stop," I said, when his exploring hand lightly squeezed my other nipple between his thumb and forefinger.

"Wasn't planning on it, darlin'."

When he stepped back after that comment, I squeaked in protest, eliciting a little chuckle from him. "We need less clothes," he said flatly.

With another hot kiss right behind my ear, he stepped around me, striding over to the bench by the door. I needed no further instruction. While he kicked off his boots, I whipped my sweatshirt off and left it on the floor behind me as I shimmied out of my sweatpants.

I happened to turn just then, and a choked sound came from him. All I had on were my panties—bright pink cotton, to be specific. Nothing amazing. More practical than anything, although I did like them to be colorful.

Wade shook his head slowly as he hooked his fist on the bottom of his T-shirt and lifted it off in one swoop, bearing his glorious chest to me. My mouth fell open, and I didn't even care. I had avoided the sight of Wade shirtless ever since he had come back to Stolen Hearts Valley. Unfortunately, here and there, I'd caught a view by accident. It was too damn hot here in the summers to expect him not to go shirtless on the worst days.

Even then, I always looked away and I never got too close. As he shifted to undo the buttons on his fly, the subtle flex of his muscled forearms practically had me drooling. Every inch of him was honed. Between his work as a first responder, an outdoor guide, and his construction work on the side, well, his body showed it. He'd transformed from the lanky boy I'd known in high school to pure, raw man. My hands itched to touch him.

I had frozen where I stood, but when his jeans dropped to the floor and he stepped out of them, my eyes dipped down to see his blatant arousal outlined by his fitted black boxer briefs. I didn't realize I was slightly chilled until he stepped closer, his warmth was like a furnace as his body came against mine.

"You know, I missed you," he murmured softly, his tone almost reverent.

Emotion rushed into the void opened by the current of desire flowing through me. I swallowed, trying to catch a breath but getting nothing more than a shallow pant, with my pulse rampaging.

"It's not like you haven't seen me," I heard myself saying, a hint of defensiveness rising up inside.

"Darlin', you know that's not what I mean."

Wade must've sensed I didn't know what to do with this

because he said nothing further, simply dipping his head and brushing his lips across mine. In a hot second, he slipped my panties over my hips, so I returned the favor with his briefs. He blazed a wet trail down my neck and captured a nipple with the warm suction of his mouth. He lifted me easily, and in two strides, was stretching us out on the bed and rolling over so I straddled his hips. I could feel the hard ridge of his arousal nestled at the apex of my thighs.

When I opened my eyes and looked down, he was adjusting the pillows behind him as he shifted up and tugged me with him. His smoldering gaze snagged mine and my heart beat with a resounding thump of recognition.

This, right here and right now, was *everything*.

Chapter Thirteen

WADE

Dani sat astride me, her sweet little body all warm and soft curves. Her skin was flushed and dewy, and I wanted to bury myself inside of her right now and stay there forever.

The past and the present had collided, shattering the walls between us. I was still reeling inside from finally understanding what had torn her away from me. But somehow, I sensed the only way Dani could get through to the other side of this moment was in *this*. This raw, fierce, unapologetic desire that beat with its own pulse between us.

It spun around us like a tornado, catching us in its vortex with the intensity overwhelming. My cock was so hard, I nearly ached from it. I wanted to slow this down, to draw it out, but I knew that would have to wait. It was too fast and too fierce, a force well beyond my control.

I slid my hand up her spine, levering her toward me, growling in satisfaction at the feel of her bare breasts pressing against my chest, her nipples taut and her skin soft as silk. Dani shifted her hips slightly, her slick core gliding over my cock. I gritted my teeth and clung to my control.

Much as my body wanted me to rush this, I didn't want to ruin it and have it be a fumbled mad dash.

"Easy," I murmured as I moved a hand down to grab the side of her hip. I loved the soft give of her flesh under my fingers.

Even more, I loved the low sound of protest that came from her throat. She nipped at the side of my neck and lifted her head, her eyes dark with desire.

"I don't want to be easy," she replied, her voice husky and her mouth curling in a saucy smile.

I slid my tongue along my teeth, closing my eyes for a beat. It felt so good, *so* fucking good, to be with her. My eyes flew open when she shifted her hips again, letting out a little satisfied hum. Much as I wanted to drag this out and savor every moment, the beat of desire was driving us forward relentlessly. It had been too long and my body was too greedy.

"Hold up," I bit out when she rocked her hips back and forth, slicking my cock with the juices of her arousal.

"You're not about put the brakes on this," she teased, lifting her chin slightly.

"I just need a condom."

Dani's eyes widened, and she shimmied her hips back. I didn't want to contemplate what was passing through her mind just then. Rolling to the side, I reached for my jeans, which were in a rumple on the floor beside the bed. I hadn't planned it that way, but I thanked God they were within easy reach.

In a few seconds, I fumbled my wallet out and flung it to the floor once I yanked out the single emergency condom I kept in there. Dani's head bumped into mine as she leaned forward to give me an assist. The feel of her fingers curling around my cock as she rolled it on nearly made me come instantly.

I was well past the age where I rushed sex. But the moment she rose up again and the soaked heat of her core teased over my cockhead, I leaned into the pillows and gripped her hips tightly, flexing up just as she sank down.

She let out a little soft sigh, the sound spinning around me. "Ah," I rasped. "Fuck, Dani, you feel so good."

My words were slurred, and I felt drunk—drunk on the feel of Dani surrounding me. She was soft and lush in my lap, a bundle of curves. Her dewy skin pressed against mine, her full breasts bounced slightly as she shifted her hips, and the feel of her silken sheath rippled around me.

She was tight, so tight I worried I might be hurting her. When she let out a ragged moan, I asked, "You okay?"

Her eyes met mine in the dim light, the look there slicing right to my core—so open, so unguarded, so vulnerable, and so needy. The sheer force of desire I saw reflected in her gaze echoed inside of my own heart.

"Oh, I'm okay," she gasped, rocking her hips slightly before rising up to slide down over me.

Whatever I meant to say next was lost in a rough groan when she did it again. Then, we were moving as one—each time she lifted her hips, I arched up to meet her. I could feel her quickening as her channel clenched around my cock. Reaching between us at the slick fusion of our joining, I teased my fingers over the hood of her clit, exerting a slight pressure. I nearly lost control at the mere sound of her flying apart.

"Oh God, Wade, don't stop!" she ordered as her entire body trembled and she clamped tightly around me. I tumbled over the edge right after her, my release slamming through me.

Dani collapsed against me, dipping her head and tucking it inside my neck. I loved the feel of her, soft and warm in my arms. I held her close and tried to catch my breath.

Seeing as I never expected this to happen, I had no roadmap for how to react once the undeniable force of our desire had run its course.

I simply held her and remembered how right it felt to be with her.

Chapter Fourteen

DANI

"Yoo-hoo, Dani?" Valentina said from across my desk.

I gave my head a shake and looked over at her. "I'm sorry, I was totally zoning out."

Valentina's blue eyes took on a sly gleam when she smiled. "Um, yeah, I noticed. Anything going on?"

Oh, there was something going on, all right. Namely, I could hardly stop mentally replaying my encounter with Wade the other night. He'd always been a big man, but I hadn't counted on just how thoroughly he could crowd out everything else in my mind.

I shook my head, ignoring the slight disappointment that flitted across Valentina's face. We had accounting to focus on. That was more important than me obsessing about Wade, that was for sure.

"Okay, where are we at?" I asked.

Valentina launched into a review of the latest numbers for the accounts for the rescue program and the vet clinic. I mostly handled everything associated with the lodge and the restaurant, while Valentina handled the rest and did the bookkeeping for everything. Thank goodness.

I could be a control freak, but I was way too busy to manage all of that stuff. Not to mention I wasn't technically an accountant. I did my best, but Valentina actually knew her shit and had tightened things up significantly since we brought her on.

I managed to pay attention for maybe ten minutes.

"Yoo-hoo, Dani?" Valentina repeated.

Looking down, I noticed I had just doodled Wade's name with two hearts on either side of it in pencil on my desk calendar. Sweet Jesus. I was in trouble.

"Sorry," I said with an apologetic smile.

Valentina regarded me for a moment, tucking one of her pretty red curls behind her ear. Valentina was ridiculously beautiful, in my opinion. With her dark-red hair, her wide blue eyes, freckled cheeks, and her curvy body, most men had a hard time *not* looking at her. Ever since she and Lucas had fallen in love, most of the guys around here did a better job of keeping the staring to a minimum. Lucas was so head over heels in love with her, it was almost like a fairytale.

Although Valentina was a newer friend, seeing as I hadn't known her until she took her position here, I'd grown to adore her, and I trusted her implicitly. She was one of those people who had a wise old-soul quality to her. She put the computer tablet she was holding on my desk and leaned over. I didn't get my hand over Wade's name fast enough.

"Ha! I knew it!" she exclaimed with a flourish as she leaned back. "If you and Wade are finally going to stop dancing around each other, that'll be the best news ever."

My cheeks heated as I eyed her. Wrinkling my nose, I tried to glare at her, but it was weak, and I knew it. "Please don't give me hell about this."

I was trying to keep my tone light, but the baggage that I carried around Wade was so fucking heavy.

Valentina's eyes softened. "Okay, I won't tease. Wanna talk?" she asked earnestly.

I surprised myself by replying, "That might be a good idea."

Valentina smiled, so pleased with herself that I couldn't help but laugh. "Oh, I forgot, girlfriends are new for you."

Prior to moving here to Stolen Hearts Lodge, Valentina's life had been sheltered by her devout parents who did their darnedest to keep her wrapped in a bubble. As such, now that she was out on her own, she loved having friends and chatting. She even liked to be the subject of gossip. She told us it made her feel like her life was worth gossiping about.

Narrowing my eyes, I added, "Just keep in mind not all of us enjoy being the subject of gossip."

Valentina's eyes widened slightly as she shook her head. "I would never. Unless I knew you wanted me too," she added with a grin. Sobering, she went quiet for a few beats, her gaze considering. "Here, I'm just gonna tell you what I think. Wade's in love with you. And, I'm not sure what happened between you two, but it's obvious he means something to you as well. I'm not just saying that because you wrote hearts around his name."

I put my face in my hands and groaned. "I can't believe you saw that."

When I looked up, Valentina lifted a shoulder in a small shrug. "Nothing to be embarrassed about. I've put hearts around Lucas's name. I even practiced writing my name with his last name. Then, I questioned it because while I want to marry him, I shouldn't just automatically plan to take his name, right?"

Her question was dead serious, so I replied honestly. "I think feminism means women choose what they want to do when it comes to things like that. It's all about having the power to make the choice. If you want to keep your last name, do it. If you want to take Lucas's last name, do it. If you want to do the hyphenated thing, do that. You two each only have single syllable last names, so it wouldn't be too much of a mouthful."

Valentina eyed me for a moment and then picked up a pencil off of my desk, leaning over to write on my calendar *Valentina Smith-Cole*. Underneath that, she wrote *Valentina Cole-Smith*. She cocked her head to the side as she considered her handiwork. "Hmmm? I'll have to think about that."

"Good thing is, Lucas is so in love with you, he won't even care. In fact, if you asked him to take your last name, he'd probably happily do it."

Valentina's return smile was bright as the sun. "You know, I think you're right. Although, that might be confusing for Rylie, so we have to consider that."

"You're a good egg," I replied.

"Why do you say that?"

"Because you don't even have to think to put Rylie's needs first. That's not the case for everybody when it's not their own child."

Valentina nodded. "Rylie's so precious to me. I know technically she's not mine, but in every way that matters, it feels like she is." At my nod, she continued, "So, let's not get caught up on me. You and Wade. What's going on?"

"Promise you won't say anything?"

Valentina held a palm up with a solemn nod.

On the heels of a deep breath, I opened with, "I think I might have made a big mistake."

"Why?"

"I spent the night with Wade two nights ago."

"Does 'spent the night' mean you had sex?"

Even though it made my cheeks catch fire, I nodded.

"Well, that's great, right? I mean, he totally has the hots for you."

I leaned back in my chair with a sigh, looking up at the ceiling as I spun my chair slowly in a circle before coming back around to face Valentina. "I don't know. It's complicated."

"Everyone's complicated, all by themselves. Throw

another person in the mix, and it just gets even messier," Valentina observed.

"Can I ask you something?"

"Anything."

"If you knew someone wanted to have kids, and you knew that you might not be able to have kids, do you think it's fair to let things go somewhere?"

Okay, so, I hadn't planned on asking that question. Our conversation got serious in a big fat hurry. My heart was thudding in a sick beat and my stomach was busy tying itself in knots.

Valentina didn't miss a beat. Her gaze sobered, and she cocked her head to the side. "That's not an easy answer. I think the only thing you need to do is be honest. I feel like I'm missing something kinda big here."

"You mean, you might be wondering why I'm asking." The laugh that followed my words was slightly bitter. "To make a very long story short, I got pregnant the one and only time I had sex with Wade, when I was seventeen. We even used a condom, but it still happened. It turned out to be an ectopic pregnancy and I almost bled to death when I miscarried. The doctors told me at the time that I was at higher risk of having another ectopic pregnancy as a result of that. They told me I should be careful and be prepared for the fact that I might not be able to have children."

My words came out in a rapid spill, although my tone was flat as if it were a story I'd recited thousands of times. I supposed it was. I'd certainly recited it to myself that many, and more. Valentina was silent as she considered me. I suddenly wanted to cry, tears stinging hot in my eyes and my throat clogging tight with emotion.

Valentina moved quickly, standing and coming around the desk to lean over and pull me into a warm hug. When she drew back, there was nothing but understanding in her eyes. "That's so scary, and I'm so sorry."

I sniffled and swiped at my tears. She snagged a tissue

and handed it to me. After I wiped my eyes and blew my nose, she held my gaze. "Do you want to know what I think?" I nodded. "I think you should talk to Wade about it, if that's what's holding you back."

I felt half-crazy. I'd spent so much time and energy not allowing myself to ever hope for anything between Wade and me. Now, it was like a river rushing through a dam that had just opened. It wasn't simply desire. It was a tangle of emotion, want, need, and raw craving—physical and emotional. All of it spun into the intense connection I felt with him that undergirded everything.

"How do you know kids are really important to Wade?" Valentina rounded my desk again to sit down across from me. "Don't take this the wrong way, but it doesn't seem like you would've had a conversation with him about it," she said slowly, almost tentatively.

I laughed softly, that old bitterness tightening in my heart. "True. It's not something we've talked about in the last few years. But I knew when he was younger that he loved kids. That's all."

"Just because he loves kids doesn't mean he wants them. It seems to me you might be trying to find a deal breaker."

"A deal breaker?"

Her curls bounced with her nod. "Yeah. A deal breaker. You know, something that makes it so you two can't be together. I understand that it's scary, but there's only one thing to do. Give him a chance, or not."

Staring at her, I actually had to grit my teeth to keep from snapping at her. I could have a bit of a temper, but I always felt bad if I snapped at Valentina. She was too earnest.

After a steadying breath, I shrugged, aiming for nonchalance. "I'm not trying to find a deal breaker. And I'm not scared," I muttered.

Just then, the phone on my desk rang. "I need to take

this," I said quickly, grabbing onto the lifeline of this interruption.

Valentina was too kind to let on that she might know better. She stood quickly, reaching for the computer tablet and closing the case as she replied, "Of course. We can check in tomorrow about these numbers. I'll email you the spreadsheets, and you can let me know if you have any questions."

I was nodding and answering the phone at the same time, relieved when she turned and walked briskly out of my office, closing the door behind her. I took the call, only half-paying attention. After I hung up, I leaned my elbows on my desk and rested my face in my hands, letting out a soft sigh. My breath filtered through my fingers before I brushed my hands through my hair, pointlessly attempting to tidy my usually unruly curls.

Normally, I liked having my office door open. It meant people could bounce in and out whenever they needed. I loved the hustle and bustle of managing the restaurant here at the lodge and worked to create a sense of family for everyone who worked here. Right now though, I didn't stand and go to open my door as I typically would after I got off the phone.

Even though there was not a soul in this room with me, I felt exposed, worried that anyone who knew me could see how unsettled I was inside. I was an idiot. I had given in and told Wade the whole messy story. I felt as if he were slipping in through the cracks in the walls around my heart.

My mind flashed back to the other night. His espresso gaze holding mine as I sank down over him. The delicious stretch of him filling me. His easy strength, the way he just didn't care for me to be anything other than who I was. Even with all of our baggage and complications, once I let my guard down with Wade, it all came so easily.

I should have made him leave, found some graceful way to say good night. But I hadn't been able to force the issue. I had fallen asleep with his strong arms wrapped around me. I'd been beyond relieved when he woke up in the early dawn to brush a kiss against my cheek as he said goodbye. He had training in Asheville and an overnight winter camping trip for a small group an hour away.

The dusting of his lips against my cheek and the soft, open-mouthed kiss he pressed against that sweet spot right behind my ear sent shivers all the way through me and made me deeply understand the meaning of longing. Yet, I'd been relieved to know I would have two days to try to pull myself together.

Those two days hadn't helped at all. If anything, my longing for Wade had grown sharper in its intensity.

Chapter Fifteen

WADE

"Hey!" Lucas called as Rylie came flying across the room and flung herself at him.

Lucas caught his daughter easily, lifting her high and setting her on his hip. Their matching dark hair glinted under the lights above.

Lucas said something to her, and Rylie nodded before looking toward Jackson and me. "Hi," she said with a bright smile.

"Hey, Rylie girl," I drawled. "Looks like you might've lost a tooth."

Rylie's smile widened. "I sure did, and the tooth fairy only gave me a dollar." Rylie's eyes angled back up to her father. "And Daddy is terrible at pretending like he's not the tooth fairy."

Jackson lost the battle at holding back his laugh.

"Do tell," I said as I looked from Rylie to Lucas.

Lucas smiled sheepishly. "I don't know, but I guess I'm considered cheap."

Rylie giggled, bumping her elbow into Lucas's ribs. "My friend got two dollars. I only got one. So, I told Daddy the tooth fairy didn't like me as much. Then, I caught him sneaking in to give me more money the next night." Rylie tsk-tsked her father. "So, then he had to explain the tooth fairy isn't real." Rylie added an elaborate eye roll to this.

I laughed, leaning my elbow on the counter that surrounded the reception desk at the vet clinic. "Well, did you get more money out of it?"

Rylie nodded vigorously. "Sure did. I got two whole dollars."

Shay came walking down the hallway, her eyes lighting up when she saw Rylie and Lucas. "Hey you!" She hurried over and lifted Rylie from Lucas's arms. As soon as she did, she groaned. "Honey, you're almost too big for me to pick up."

"I'm six," Rylie chirped, as if that explained everything when Shay lowered her feet to the floor. Rylie dashed down the hallway. "Valentine!"

Lucas chuckled. "I don't think she's ever going to stop calling her Valentine."

"Who cares?" I countered.

"I sure don't," Lucas replied. "I'm gonna follow her down there." With a quick grin, he turned and jogged to catch up to his daughter.

Shay walked behind the reception counter, glancing over to Jackson and me. "You boys want some coffee?"

Jackson nodded. "Yes, please. Been a long day."

"I'll always take a coffee," I added when Shay flicked her gaze toward me.

"Coming right up then."

While Shay started prepping the coffee, Jackson ran a hand through his shaggy brown curls, looking toward me. "So, how was the winter hike?"

"Fucking cold."

Jackson chuckled, his blue eyes crinkling at the corners. "Yeah, I don't mind the cold so much. But, I don't really understand people fucking paying us to lead them on eight-mile hikes when the weather's like that," he said, nudging his chin toward the window where an icy rain was falling outside.

"Same here," I replied. Looking down, I idly noted the mud on my boots and considered that a hot shower after an eight-mile hike and cold damp weather was a special kind of heaven.

At that moment, Boone came walking through the front doors. "Hey, y'all," he said as he crossed the room to us.

Shay turned as the soft drip of the coffee pot began and cast Boone a smile. "I wouldn't do it," she said as she rested her elbows on the counter opposite from Jackson.

"Wouldn't do what?" Boone asked when he stopped beside me.

"Pay someone to take me on a hike in the winter."

Boone chuckled and shrugged. "Do I get some of that coffee?"

"Of course. You don't even have to ask," Shay replied.

Jackson smiled at her and reached over to lightly tug on her long blonde ponytail. Her cheeks pinkened slightly before she leaned over and pressed a kiss to his cheek.

"That's all I get?" he teased when she pulled back.

She grinned. "Yes. We have an audience and you have one more appointment this afternoon," she said, then turned away to check on the coffee pot.

Between Lucas and Valentina's fresh love, in addition to Jackson and Shay's and Dawson and Evie's, the rest of us working around the lodge were getting accustomed to the PDA. Most of the time, I shrugged it off.

Ever since the other night, I wished I could have that kind of easy affection with Dani. I only hoped she hadn't battened down the hatches again and reinforced her walls in the days I'd been gone.

At that moment, Rylie came dashing back down the hallway and skidded around the corner of the reception desk. Reflexively, I turned and caught her in my arms, lifting her high. She squealed as I set her down, laughing when I ruffled her hair.

Lucas and Valentina were right behind her, following at a more sedate pace. Valentina smiled over at me. "You're so good with kids."

"Yeah, that's why Wade's in charge of all the school trips here," Jackson offered with a wry chuckle.

I shrugged. "I don't mind a bit. Y'all know my mom ran a daycare, so I was surrounded by kids."

All true, and I *did* love kids. Just then, my mind spun back to the little bomb about what Dani had told me. A shaft of pain struck me, my heart giving an achy thump. With so many missing pieces of the puzzle finally falling into place, in some ways, I felt better. Understanding was a comfort. And yet, I also felt worse. I hated what she went through. Part of me was relieved her father was dead. Otherwise, I'd have been hard-pressed not to give him hell.

I felt helpless to repair what had happened. As much as Dani had let go with me the other night, I knew I had run a risk. Even without knowing the complicated history of pain she carried around, I didn't know why she felt forced to cut me out of her life and the frightening experience of having a miscarriage like that. But then, Dani had always had a prickly side.

She loved hard and was fiercely loyal, but she didn't let people in easily. Perhaps it was because her father had always been emotionally distant. Hell, I had no clue just how emotionally distant he'd been. I wanted to shake him and tell him I'd been half in love with his daughter at the time. I had literally been counting the days for when she would come back home that summer.

I wished I hadn't fallen into my own place tinged with bitterness. When I came back to Stolen Hearts Valley and Jackson offered me a job here, it was a natural fit with my position on the first responder crew. The only rub had been I knew Dani would be pissed. Yet, all that time, I thought her secret was something about another guy. Or that she just didn't like me as much as I'd liked her. Or, or, or. I hadn't let myself dwell on it, not after that last year of high school.

Of all the possibilities, I hadn't counted on what the story actually was. I wanted my second chance with Dani.

Just as I was zoning out, Shay nudged my elbow from across the reception counter. "Coffee," she said. I looked down to see her passing over a mug of black coffee. "You don't like anything in it, right?"

"No, this is perfect." I lifted the mug and took a hearty swallow.

The front entrance to the vet clinic opened and a family came in with a very wiggly puppy bounding on a long lead. Right behind the puppy and family was Dani, her arms laden with boxes of Christmas lights spilling out every which way.

Grace was walking with Dani. I felt the tension pick up. Fortunately, most eyes went to the puppy happily bounding about the waiting area after he slipped the grip on his lead.

"Oh, awesome!" Shay exclaimed as she came around from behind the reception area, setting her coffee on the counter and hurrying over to fetch a box of lights from Dani.

Jackson approached and snagged the puppy's lead. He said something to the little girl before greeting the mother.

Grace quickly looked away from Boone when he glanced in her direction as he took a swallow of his coffee. She walked over to a row of chairs against the wall and set down the box of lights in her arms while Shay and Dani followed her.

Shay glanced over to Boone and me, commenting, "Please tell me you'll stay and help for a little bit. We could use the height."

For just a second, I considered whether Dani would want that, but I quickly decided it didn't matter. I would help, and maybe, just maybe, I would get a chance to talk to Dani afterwards.

"Of course I'll help," I replied, letting my gaze travel to

Dani when she turned at the sound of Jackson calling Shay's name.

While Shay hurried to check on something with the vet appointment, Dani's cheeks flushed pink when she met my eyes. She didn't look away, lifting her chin slightly, a stubborn tilt to it. "We can always use the help, so thanks."

"My pleasure," I replied, letting my lips kick up in a smile.

"Boone's helping too," Shay said as she returned.

Jackson disappeared down the hallway with the puppy bouncing at his side and the family following along.

If I thought there was tension between me and Dani, Grace and Boone might have one-upped us on that account. Grace eyed him suspiciously, her gaze quickly sliding away. She immediately set herself to paying diligent attention as she carefully untangled the Christmas lights in one of the boxes.

Boone offered to do whatever Shay needed. If Shay picked up on the tension, she clearly decided she was going to ignore it. I sensed she had ulterior motives here.

We all knew Grace and Boone dated once upon a time. I didn't know the details, but my recollection was the breakup was icy. In a bid to snap through the tension, I glanced to Boone. "Shall we go grab some ladders?"

Relief passed across his face as he nodded with alacrity. "Sure thing."

Chapter Sixteen

DANI

"Okay, what the hell?" I asked, keeping my voice low as I fed the Christmas lights to Shay where she stood on a stepladder.

Shay didn't spare me a glance. "What do you mean?"

"Fine. Play dumb. What's your deal with asking Wade and Boone to help? You know Grace gets super tense around Boone."

Grace was across the room, having dedicated herself to the rather tedious task of making star shapes out of the Christmas lights on one wall. Mind you, it wasn't like that was necessary, but she suggested it. It also happened to be a task she needed no assistance with, which was convenient.

Shay glanced down to me, a slow smile stretching across her face. "I'm not trying to make things difficult, but those two need to talk. What the hell happened with them anyway?" she asked. "Grace and Evie were two years behind us in high school so I didn't get all the details."

"Yeah, same here. I don't know. Something about him cheating on her. Like Wade, he moved away during college and now he's back. What is it with all these men becoming first responders and then working at this damn lodge?" I muttered, almost to myself. "Here's the end of this run." I fed up the last bit and turned to grab another section of lights.

Shay looked away as she affixed the lights under the tiny nails Wade had placed in even intervals where the wall met the ceiling. As I carefully unwound a string of lights, I glanced up at Shay. "Ready?"

"Sure am. Just keep handing them up," she replied. "To your question, this is a good place to work. It so happens most of the crew for the first responder team is friends with Jackson. So even if they don't work here, they're going to pop in every so often. Instead of worrying about Grace and Boone, why don't you tell me what's up with you and Wade?"

Shay's tone was innocent, but she didn't fool me. Not for a second. I shrugged when she looked down at me, willing my face not to flush. "Why do you ask?"

"Because for once, y'all aren't at each other's throats. Maybe you finally burned off some of that tension?" she teased as she reached for the lights I was feeding up.

As if on cue, Wade came back through the door. "How's it going in here?" he drawled. After he and Boone helped us get set up, he had left, saying he desperately needed to shower.

When I looked over, my pulse took off at a gallop. Wade's presence was like the starting shot at a race. His brown hair was damp and his skin was flushed from the cold outside. An icy gust of wind came in through the door behind him.

I saw Grace turn and look toward the door. Her expression was so controlled it was hard to know if I saw disappointment or not. My eyes immediately traveled back to Wade as if he were a magnetic point in my own personal compass.

He walked with an easy swagger, his faded jeans molded to his legs. He wore a T-shirt under an unbuttoned denim shirt. I instantly recalled the feel of his muscled chest against my body and my mouth watered as liquid heat slid through my veins.

Shay replied to Wade's question. Good thing too because, apparently, I was speechless. "We're almost done."

"Need any more tall person assistance?" he asked as he stopped beside me. The scent of fresh snow and winter air clinging to him struck me. The urge to be enveloped in his strength and his intoxicating scent was nearly overpowering.

I handed up another section of lights. Shay glanced down, commenting, "I think this is the wrong end."

Flustered, I glanced down to the two sections I held in my hands.

"Here, I'll take those," Wade said. His fingers brushed mine as he lifted one string of lights from my grip.

"Here you go," I said, sheepishly handing the other to Shay.

She gave me a knowing smile and kept working. With my hands empty, I willed myself not to look in Wade's direction, but my eyes had more say in the matter. Looking over, I saw him reaching above his head and quickly tucking the lights over the nails. I forced my eyes away only to catch Shay watching me. My ears got hot, and I knew my face was probably bright red.

"It's okay," she said under her breath, "he's totally hot. I don't blame you."

"Shut up!" I hissed before I elbowed her in the knee as she climbed down from the ladder.

She squeaked. "Hey, easy."

Looking away, I strode over to where Grace was finishing up the last star she had created. She tapped a hammer lightly on a tiny nail. "Those look great," I said as I surveyed her work.

Grace smiled over at me, her expression more relaxed than it had been earlier when Boone was here. "Thanks. I thought we might as well make it a little fun."

I spun in a slow circle, taking in the twinkling lights running along the ceiling, and Grace's wall with its collection of stars scattered across it. There were two small wreaths mounted on the double doors at the front and a large one hanging above the reception desk on the wall behind it.

"It feels festive," Shay commented as she stopped beside me.

The family came out with the puppy, effectively breaking up our little party. If that was what it was. Shay hurried over to check them out while Grace and I packed up the boxes.

Grace glanced at the clock above the door just as we were finishing up. "I need to get to the lodge for my shift," she said suddenly.

"You go on, I'll take these down to the storage room."

Grace hurried off. The moment she was gone, I realized that left me alone with Wade while Jackson and Shay walked down the hallway after the family exited out the front door.

The moment I looked at him, I was trapped in his gaze. I hated how much the hope inside my heart was trying to get my attention. I felt like it was a little cheerleader inside, throwing pom-poms in the air, doing flips, and all sorts of ridiculousness. Just to get me to believe maybe I should hope for something.

Here, I had somehow convinced myself I was strong, certainly stronger than that dark summer which stole a piece of my soul and made me wonder if my banged-up heart could ever want anyone again.

"Well, thanks for your help," I heard myself saying brightly.

Wade held my gaze. For a few seconds, I felt as if I had stepped into the past—smack into the middle of those months leading up to that one night with Wade. Months of stolen kisses, of giggles, of having a silly crush on a boy who had been my friend for years.

I had trusted Wade so completely. What I hadn't understood was that even when you trusted someone, life could still break your heart.

But for those few seconds, I was caught in his gaze, in the tractor beam of intimacy, understanding, and innocence contained there. Not because he was innocent, nor I, for that matter, but because once upon a time, life had sent us skidding sideways and we hadn't been able to see it coming. We'd clambered out of the wreckage, nursing our own wounds alone.

Tearing my eyes free from his, with my breath coming in shallow pants, I looked down at the empty boxes sitting on a chair beside me. "I have to carry these downstairs," I said, my words coming out breathy and shaky.

"I'll help," Wade said easily. If he sensed how rattled I was, he didn't let on.

I opened my mouth to protest and a slow grin stretched across his face. "Dani, you're not gonna argue with me. Not over something as small as carrying boxes."

I bit the inside of my cheeks and shook my head. "No, I was going to say thank you," I lied.

"No you weren't, but that's all right." Without waiting, he went to the boxes, quickly stacking them on top of each other and lifting them. "There, I've got them all. Just tell me where to put 'em."

I wrinkled my nose. "You know, I could've gotten all those. They're empty boxes. Not exactly heavy."

"'Course you could. But I'm helping. Lead the way," he said, gesturing with his chin toward the side door that led to the lower level of the renovated barn.

I walked ahead of him, holding the door open as he passed through with the boxes. The echo of my footsteps was loud on the wooden staircase. With this barn built into a hillside, the vet clinic and administrative offices occupied the upper floor, while the lower floor had storage on one side and horse stalls on the other. The barn downstairs was quiet this time of night.

Shay usually took care of the feeding, and I knew she had fed the horses before we came over to help with the lights because she had texted to make sure I didn't bring the lights over before she was done.

The motion sensor light came on when I stepped onto the landing at the base of the stairs. The lighting was adjusted for the time so that it wasn't too bright for the horses down here. I could hear the soft sounds of them chewing hay as I passed the aisle between the stalls.

Another light came on as I moved into the hallway beyond that where there was a row of storage rooms. This was the newest barn on the old farm property. Jackson had it built across from his family's old farmhouse where he lived with Shay now.

I was hyper-aware of Wade's presence behind me. Every hair on my body was raised slightly. It felt as if my cells themselves were standing at attention, all focused toward Wade although I wasn't even looking at him.

"In here," I said, opening a door at the end of the hallway, with another light coming on the moment I stepped into the room. Only a month ago, Shay had Jackson install motion sensor lights just about everywhere on the farm and at the lodge. She said she was tired of showing up in rooms and trying to fumble for light switches.

"Just tell me where to put them," Wade said as he stepped past me into the small storage room.

The room was lined with shelves on all sides. This space was the room equivalent of a junk drawer. The other storage rooms had more organized purposes, such as the tack room, the feed room, and so on. This one served as the catchall for things that had nowhere else to go.

"Right there," I said, pointing to an upper shelf.

Wade lifted the empty boxes and slipped them onto the shelf. My eyes, my willful eyes, dropped to the little strip of skin that peeked out as his T-shirt rose when he lifted his arms above his head. He just had to expose that strip of skin above his jeans where I could see his muscled abs and the trail of dark hair that led to the promised land.

That was what my body thought Wade's cock was. I didn't realize I had let out a little sigh until he dropped his arms and turned, his gaze immediately capturing mine.

"Now, what was that for?" he drawled.

"Just breathing," I snapped, flustered he was so attuned to me.

"Just breathing, huh?" he mused as he stepped closer, lifting a hand and catching one of my curls. He pulled it out and let it go. It bounced on my cheek.

"You're pulling my hair?"

"I don't think that quite counts as pulling your hair," he teased as he came even closer. "I bet you didn't even feel that. Not like this." Another step erased the distance between us. He trailed the backs of his fingers along my side, his touch nothing more than light and teasing.

I had to bite my lip to keep from crying out as his fingers coasted up over my shoulder and along the side of my neck, goose bumps rising in the wake of his touch. His thumb dusted gently across my jaw as his hand slid into my hair, gripping just enough that I could feel the tug on my scalp.

I feared he could see the shock of lust on my face. Oh God, why did I have to want this man so much?

"Lie to me, Dani. Tell me you don't feel that," he murmured, his tone husky, stepping so his chest was flush against mine.

My nipples were tight little peaks pressed against his chest. I wanted to wrap my arms around him and lose myself in everything that was Wade as need thundered through me.

When I looked into his eyes, that old trickle of annoyance I clung to—that had protected me so well—failed to fire up.

Chapter Seventeen

DANI

I wanted to lie, just as he demanded, but I found I couldn't. Wade, after all, wasn't the one who caused me so much pain. He was collateral damage, a reminder of what had all gone so wrong when I was too young to have the emotional fortitude to manage it well.

The playful glint in his eyes faded, and he eased his grip on my hair. His touch gentled as his hand cupped the back of my neck lightly. "What is it, baby? I see how hard you're thinking."

Emotion coursed through me, and I shook my head sharply.

"Not gonna lie?" he asked, all teasing traces gone from his voice.

"No," I whispered, letting my forehead fall against his strong and solid chest.

The boy I once fancied myself falling in love with held me as the man he was now. Somehow, he just knew talking was not the thing for me, not right now. His other arm slid around me, and he held me close as I breathed through the tears. I wasn't ready to be a crying mess in Wade's arms. Yet, here I was.

I didn't know how long we stood like that, with him holding me and his fingers lightly sifting through my curls as I breathed and marveled at how we'd gotten here.

The one man I'd tried so hard not to let my guard down with had ripped away the walls around my heart. I couldn't even figure out how to rebuild them. At least, not with him.

It was all so confusing. I never should've been angry with Wade. It was just, it all hurt so much. In hindsight, I supposed a small part of me wished he had somehow known how deeply I was hurting and that he had somehow known I needed him after that.

When I gathered myself together, I finally lifted my head, leaning back slightly to look at him. My mouth twisted to the side. "I don't know," I said because that was the only thing I could think to say.

Wade's dark eyes searched mine. "You don't have to know everything, Dani," he replied softly. "So tell me, why are we arguing about this?"

A flash of defensiveness rose inside of me, but it collapsed when I searched his gaze and realized he wasn't even teasing. He was dead serious.

I managed to gulp in a breath and shrugged, letting my forehead fall onto his chest again. It was hard to look in his eyes and keep myself together. "Because I don't like to lie," I mumbled into his chest.

Wade was quiet, his fingers sifting lightly through the curls at the base of my neck. When I finally scrambled together the nerve to lift my head, I found his gaze thoughtful.

As we looked at each other, it felt as if a storm was gathering in the sky. There was a sense of leashed energy, a humming electricity, and a quickening. Part of me was near frantic for Wade to just kiss me.

Then, I could lose myself in that madness, and I didn't

have to tolerate the sense of uncertainty and vulnerability churning inside. As if he read my mind, he ran his tongue across his teeth, sending a prickle of electric awareness up my spine.

When he dipped his head, I almost jumped at the *zing* when his lips brushed across mine. Another subtle touch of his lips to mine, and I moaned. But he pulled back quickly, and I squeaked in protest.

"What are you doing?" I demanded.

"I'm not gonna screw this up this time, Dani."

"You didn't screw up anything before," I protested.

"Maybe. That's not the point. I know you, and I know you're not sure about us. I am. This time, we're going to get it right. But I need to know we're not just something to forget yourself in. Do you understand?" he asked roughly, his dark gaze penetrating mine.

My heart felt as if it were galloping inside my chest while anxiety, stress, and uncertainty spun into each other. I felt as if I were in an elevator that had abruptly gone down, *way* too fast. My internal equilibrium was thrown into chaos, and it felt as though the ground had been ripped from under my feet.

"Wade—" I began, stopping when he shook his head slightly.

The hand curled around my nape slid forward, his thumb tracing along my jawline as he cupped my cheek. He bent low once again to press his lips to mine. He lingered just long enough that I whimpered slightly when he drew back.

"You know what I mean, baby. I know you do. I'll be waiting."

At that, his hand dropped away and he stepped back. He lightly squeezed my shoulder as he walked past me and exited the room. I stood there, frozen in place, as I listened to his footsteps move down the hallway, then the sound of the door opening and closing in the early darkness.

"Fuck you, Wade. I don't know what the hell you're talking about," I said into the silence.

My mind whispered right back. *Yes, you do. You know exactly what he means. You're terrified to let this be anything but sex.*

I took a slow, steadying breath, wishing I could slap the shit out of my internal voice. Turning, I stepped out of the storage room and closed the door behind me. My heart was still beating wildly with an uneasiness churning in my stomach. Walking down the hall, I made a U-turn into the aisle between the two rows of horse stalls. A recent rescue, Misty, nickered softly when she saw me approach.

I had fallen in love with this sweet girl and planned to talk to Shay and Jackson about keeping her around. She was a lovely Quarter Horse-Thoroughbred mix, rescued from a hoarding situation. She'd shown up here way too thin, but she was friendly and gentle.

I leaned against her stall, reaching to the side where there was a sealed bucket that held treats for anyone who happened to be passing by. After fetching a grain treat, I held it flat on my palm. She nibbled it up and leaned her head over the door to her stall. Her color was dappled gray, and she had a crooked white blaze on her nose that went down to one side.

"Hey, sweet girl," I said, scratching behind her ears and smoothing my hand down along the side of her neck.

She let out a deep sigh, hanging her head low as I continued to stroke her, admiring that she had put on a little weight. "You're looking good," I murmured, resting my forehead against the side of her neck.

I felt rattled inside, everything clanging and loud. I was finding it hard to regain the balance I had found for the last few years around Wade. Somehow, I had managed to buckle everything up tight, to keep my feelings contained. Now, they were all over the place.

I didn't like it. I wanted my emotions to be something I

could manage, something I could control. If there was one thing that God-awful summer had taught me, it was that feeling out of control sucked. Having my father tell me what I could and couldn't do had made me feel beyond helpless. Almost dying from a miscarriage had been utterly terrifying. The fear that gripped me when I realized I was pregnant had felt like a boulder rushing toward me from above. I'd gone out of my way ever since then to keep everything in my life buttoned down and under control.

When Misty lifted her head, nickering softly once more before turning to nibble on some hay, I finally pushed away from her stall and walked out of the barn. Just as I stepped outside, leaving behind the quiet and peaceful barn, the sound of Jackson calling Wade's name nearly made me jump out of my skin.

With nearly half the members of Stolen Hearts Valley Emergency Response team living and working here at the lodge, they kept an emergency vehicle on site, parked by the vet clinic. Glancing over, I saw Dawson and Jackson convening at the truck and then Wade jogged out from the path where his cabin was, flinging his bag over his shoulder. On his heels came Walker Hudson, a new guy around the lodge. He seemed nice enough, but I didn't know him well.

My heart started kicking along in an anxious, choppy beat as I watched them clamber into the emergency vehicle. Gravel spun behind the tires as they took off into the darkness. They didn't turn the siren on until they hit the end of the long, winding driveway that led to the lodge and farm.

I shouldn't have been all worked up. For three freaking years, I'd been working at this lodge. On any given day, I knew perfectly well some of my friends were putting their lives on the line when they got called out to an emergency.

But now? Now I was all stirred up, worrying something might happen to Wade. I was still frozen in place where I'd skidded to a stop moments ago, and belatedly realized I'd left my jacket upstairs in the clinic.

Shivering, I hurried back into the barn and jogged up the stairs to the clinic. When I got upstairs, Shay was spraying disinfectant on the reception counter. The lights were dimmed, and the space was quiet.

"That was a quick appointment," I commented as I crossed the room toward her.

Shay paused before looking back and giving another squirt with the bottle of disinfectant. "It was just a check-up and a round of shots. Jackson can handle those in about five minutes. Especially if no one's flirting with him," she explained with a chuckle.

I managed a smile even though worry was spinning in tight circles in my chest. "You're quite patient with his many admirers."

She shrugged. "Hazards of the job, right? Sometimes it's annoying."

"It's not like you ever need to worry. Jackson adores you."

She finished wiping the end of the counter and tossed the paper towel into the trash can by the wall. Turning and resting her hips against the back of the counter, she flashed a shy smile. "I don't worry. I was just teasing."

"Good. Because that man loves you. And you two have known each other long enough that I think it's fair to say it's going to stick."

Shay's cheeks flushed slightly. "I sure hope so."

"So, what's the call about?" I asked, my impatience to know winning the battle against my attempt to be rational.

Shay's eyes narrowed slightly, but blessedly, she answered. "It's a car accident. Roads are icy tonight because it warmed up. A little melting on these mountain roads, and that means black ice at night." She sighed. "I try not to worry. You know?"

When she leveled her gaze with mine, I managed a nod and hoped I looked calm and normal. Unfortunately, inside, my heartbeat zoomed along at an unsteady pace and my stomach was knotted. I knew this wasn't rational.

"Hey, are you okay?" Shay asked as she pushed away from the counter. She lifted a hand and ran it over my shoulder, squeezing lightly at my elbow.

I tried to take a deep breath and calm the irregular beat of my heart, but it was to no avail. When I was a little girl, my mother used to tease that my emotions were always written in magic marker on my face. About now—well, just about any time I didn't want someone to know what I was thinking or feeling—I hated that.

I finally shook my head. "I think I'm going a little crazy." Stepping forward, I leaned my elbows on the counter. Resting my face in my hands, I muttered, "Fuck." I tried to take several soothing breaths, but my lungs weren't cooperating.

Tunneling my hands through my curls, I smoothed them back as I straightened and glanced down, noticing my elbows left dusty smudges on the counter. I looked over at Shay. "Sorry, I just got your clean counter dirty. I was just downstairs petting Misty. Promise me y'all will keep her." I was all about distractions, and discussing a sweet rescue horse was perfect.

Shay's lips quirked in a small smile. "I already talked to Jackson. She's got such a good temperament. He's on board. As for the counter, it's no biggie. Tell me why you're going crazy."

"I think I need a drink for this," I said bluntly, swallowing against the emotion tightening my chest and hoping the tears I felt stinging my eyes didn't break free.

"Okay then. Let me grab my jacket." Shay blessedly didn't comment further.

While Shay jogged down to the hallway to her office, I got a clean paper towel from behind the desk and quickly sprayed the disinfectant on the counter again. It probably wasn't necessary, but she *had* just finished cleaning.

In another moment, she returned. "Shall we go to the

staff kitchen? Or over to Jackson's place?" Shay asked as we reached the front door.

Sliding my gaze to her, I said, "For starters, you need to start calling it your place. You live there."

Shay rolled her eyes. "I'm not used to it. Give me some time."

"Fine. As for where we go, I don't really care. Wherever the wine is. I know there's plenty over at the staff kitchen."

"Now that you mention it, we're all out. It's on my grocery list. You think anyone else is over in the staff kitchen right now?" she asked as she fell into step beside me.

"Doubtful. The restaurant's in full swing right now, so it's probably quiet back there. Plus, we can always hide out in my office if we feel like it."

Our breath misted in the air as we walked between the section of the old farm to where the lodge and restaurant were. The icy rain had temporarily stopped, but it didn't make the air any warmer. We crested a small rise through the trees and the lights from the lodge came into view. It was blazing bright downstairs, with the parking lot at capacity and cars spilling out into the driveway.

Every time I thought about how busy it was, I felt a surge of pride. I loved running the restaurant. I loved to cook, and I finally had a restaurant where I could put my skills to work after having done a stint in a culinary school in New York City after college.

It was also fun being in charge, and I considered myself a benevolent boss. The role suited my personality quite well. I'd never done well answering to others, and Jackson just let me be. Although Ash was hardly ever around these days, when she was, she did too.

Shay and I stepped in through the back door, warmth enveloping us. As I'd predicted, this section of the kitchen was empty. When the restaurant was that busy, the only time anybody would run back here was if they needed something from the pantry.

While Shay fetched us some wine, I poked around in our staff refrigerator to see what leftovers we had. Finding almost half a pan of lasagna, I called over my shoulder, "Are you okay if I reheat lasagna to go with our wine?"

"Hell yeah," Shay called in reply. "I take it we'll go with a red wine for that then."

"Perfect," I replied. "I'm just gonna toss it in the microwave and sneak up front to see if we have any fresh garlic bread."

Hurrying into the restaurant kitchen, I caught one of the line cook's eyes and mouthed, "Garlic bread."

He grinned, nudging his coworker in the side. The other guy spun to quickly to snag one of the loaves wrapped in foil and waiting in the warming section of the oven.

Chapter Eighteen

DANI

Not much later, Shay and I were seated across from each other at the large picnic-style table in the back. The muted hum of the cacophony from the restaurant kitchen and the restaurant was our background music.

I took a bite of my lasagna and sighed. I was so discombobulated I hadn't even noticed I was starving.

Shay groaned as she finished a bite. "I think lasagna's one of those foods that's better reheated."

"Oh yeah. The flavors mesh better with a little time. It's even better with a second round in the oven, but I wasn't up for waiting for that."

I snagged a piece of the garlic bread, which was buttered generously and sprinkled with real crushed garlic, parsley, and Parmesan cheese. After eating quietly for a few moments, Shay set her fork down and lasered me with her gaze.

"So, are you okay? Because I'm pretty sure you almost cried back there. There's absolutely nothing wrong with crying, but you're not really a crier."

Shay's prescience at giving me the space I needed during

our walk here had helped me corral my emotions back under my control. I chuckled and took a big gulp of my wine. "No, I'm not much of a crier." I decided to just dive right in, damn the consequences and my pride. "I had sex with Wade."

She had just taken a sip of her wine and sputtered, spewing some on the table. Wordlessly, I handed her a napkin. She dabbed at her mouth while I used another napkin to wipe up the spattered wine. "I guess I surprised you, huh?"

Shay took a deep breath before straightening and folding her hands on her lap. "Um, yeah, you startled me. I know I've been kind of teasing about you and Wade, and so has everyone else. But I didn't think something would actually happen."

I shrugged sheepishly. "Yeah, me neither. I'm kind of freaking out. Something about that call tonight just threw me off." I needed more wine, so I grabbed my glass and took another gulp, completely draining it.

Shay helpfully passed over the bottle. "So, here's what happened …" I began, stumbling through a quick summary of the events and my history with Wade. By the time I got to the part where I ended up in the hospital, I actually felt calmer. Perhaps because I'd finally said it all out loud to more than one person.

Shay's mouth dropped open, her eyes worried, with a little wrinkle in her brow. "Oh my God. That's awful."

"Yeah, it was awful and scary. My mom was great. My dad, well, he's pretty old-school, or he was. I didn't really feel like I had anyone to talk to. I was so young, and it's not the kind of thing you want to talk about, you know?"

Shay was quiet as she looked over at me. "If anyone can understand the category of things people don't really want to talk about, it's me. You know my past." She sighed and shook her head slowly.

"I know you get it. I guess maybe that's why I didn't plan on it, but I just dumped this in your lap."

"As awful as what I went through was, I was older, so I can't even imagine how scary that must've been for you."

"Shay, your ex almost beat you to death, and it was all over the news," I said flatly. Her ex-boyfriend was the son of a high-profile politician in North Carolina who had, in fact, almost beaten her to death. He was in jail—not because of that, but because he killed two people in a drunk driving accident a mere two weeks after his last assault against Shay.

She cocked her head to the side, her gaze somber. "I know. But if there's one thing I've learned about life, it's that everything is relative. Truly. What happened to me was high profile because I was in the news and that was horrifying. But you were only seventeen and your father gave you hell for accidentally getting pregnant. Then, you had an ectopic pregnancy and almost bled to death. I don't think it's about comparing the awfulness of things. It's about realizing that we're all at different places at different points in life. Life is fucking hard sometimes."

I took a deep breath, letting it out slowly. "Yeah, I know you're right. I don't know why I'm all so fucked up about Wade. I saw him going out on that call, and I had a near panic attack that something was going to happen to him."

"Oh, I get that feeling sometimes. However, I don't think that's what's important right now. I'm trying to figure out how you feel about Wade. Is this an overdue you-have-to-get-it-out-of-your-system thing? Or something else?"

"I wish I knew. Plus, none of that before was his fault. I feel like he was kind of collateral damage. And get this. We had, I guess what you might call a heated moment earlier tonight. He put the brakes on everything and told me he needed to know we're not just something I forget myself in. Whatever the hell that means," I muttered before taking a healthy swallow of wine.

Shay's grin stretched slowly across her face. "Oh wow.

He's totally putting the ball in your court. You know what I think?"

"No, but I'm guessing you're going to tell me," I mumbled, even though I was smiling.

"Hey, don't give me hell for giving you my opinion. You do it all the time."

"I know, I know," I said with a wave of my hand. "Carry on. Please tell me what you think."

"I think Wade knows you better than you think. I love this about you"—she paused to reach over and give my hand a comforting squeeze—"but you like to be in control. He's giving you all the control. You have to decide what you want to do with that."

As I stared at her, I felt my mouth slowly drop open. "Oh my God. I hate saying this, but I think you might be right."

She cackled as she paused to fill her glass of wine. My heart started doing that wild, funny beat again just thinking about Wade.

Once again, when Shay looked over, she read my face like the fucking open book it was. "Hey, I'm just teasing. You don't need to panic."

"But that's the thing. I *am* panicking."

"Okay, maybe you need to figure out how to calm down. This is not an emergency."

I leaned forward, resting my chin in my hands as I let out a sigh. "I know it's not an emergency, but I don't know what to do."

"Do you want Wade?" Shay asked bluntly.

"Yeah. I'm just afraid." The minute that word came out, I almost cringed at the understanding contained in her gaze.

"Aren't we all?" she mused. "You're so, I don't know, bitchy around him that I think his only defense is to tease back. But his teasing is like a little boy with a girl he likes. I don't think you need to be afraid he won't care."

I bit my lip, fighting the urge to smile. As much as it chafed my ego, I loved that Shay thought Wade liked me.

She took a long swallow of her wine, swirling the glass in her hand as she eyed me before setting it on the table. "You have an assignment."

"An assignment?"

Shay leaned her elbows on the table and nodded slowly, a glint entering her gaze. "You're always giving people assignments, so I'm giving you one. Figure out what you want, and go for it."

"It sounds like you think you already know what I want," I protested, rather feebly.

She lifted a shoulder in a nonchalant shrug. "I think you have unfinished business with Wade, and it's not just about sex."

Chapter Nineteen

WADE

Three crazy days passed by in a blink. Only minutes after I made it back to my cabin after my little encounter with Dani in the storage room at the barn, we'd gotten a call to a car accident that had our entire team, and two other teams from nearby towns, tied up well into the night.

By some fucking miracle, but for the grace of God, as my mother would surely say, no one had actually died in that nasty car accident. Because it happened on an icy curve, the two cars originally involved ballooned to four as other vehicles came around the corner too fast and hit that same icy patch on the road.

Everyone in every car ended up at the hospital, but we'd already gotten the update that they were all on the mend. After collapsing into bed well past three in the morning, I'd woken at six for a planned trip with Jackson and Walker to pick up a ton of supplies for the rescue program and the first responder team. Walker was new around here, and Jackson wanted to make sure we all spent time with him to help him mesh with the crew.

So far, he fit in seamlessly. He was a damn hard worker

and didn't hesitate to step up when asked. And so it had gone, for the next three days straight. Just now, I was striding back to my cabin after another emergency call, this one far more minor.

It was late, I was cold, and an icy rain was falling. As I walked past the lodge, the festive lights hanging everywhere failed to cheer me. I was exhausted and cranky, and I hadn't had a chance to see Dani except for brief, passing interactions in the last few days. She was never far from my thoughts, but I was starting to wonder if I had played my cards too soon.

I couldn't exactly say why, but with Christmas coming, I wanted something to shift with her. Stopping on my porch, I gave my raincoat a shake before pushing my door open. I was so tired I hadn't even registered that my lights were on. I didn't make a habit of leaving the lights on and wondered what the hell I'd been thinking when I left.

When I looked up, I found Dani standing over in the small kitchen area. My boots came to a stop as I stared at her, utterly disarmed by her unexpected presence. I didn't realize I'd left the door open behind me until she hurried across the room. She quickly shut it and immediately started fussing over me.

Getting past my shock, I watched, bemused, as she tugged off my wet raincoat and looked down at my boots before letting out a sigh.

"You're soaking wet. Were you using your hood?" she asked, gesturing vaguely in the direction of my head.

I ran my hand over my head, finding my hair was quite damp. I shrugged. "Wasn't thinking."

As she turned to hang up my raincoat on the hooks by the door, I leaned over to unlace my leather boots. My fingers just wouldn't cooperate, likely due to the cold, damp weather I'd been operating in for the last few hours. Next thing I knew, Dani was swatting my hands out of the way.

"You're practically on the verge of hypothermia." She

knelt down and took care of my boots. "Are you going to fall over kicking those off?" she asked as she straightened in front of me.

With her hands on her hips and her brown curls pulled into a messy bun, my heart gave a decisive kick. She was so damn cute.

Leaning forward, I let my forehead fall into the curve where her shoulder met her neck and breathed her in. She was warm, and she smelled like cinnamon and sugar.

"Did you make cookies today?" I asked, my voice muffled in her shoulder.

She giggled, the sound sending joy spinning around my heart. "I did. Can you guess what kind?"

"Something with cinnamon."

She giggled again, putting her hands on my shoulders and pushing me back. "Babe, you're heavy and I really think you need to get in the shower and warm up. Like, now."

I lifted my head, fighting back the urge to comment on the fact she'd just called me babe. The truth was, I was the kind of cold you feel in your bones. Dealing with the icy rain coming down at a steady clip while our team worked on the heels of the last three days of exhaustion had tipped me over the edge.

I stepped back and discovered I was coordinated enough to toe my boots off. Kicking them to the side, I met her gaze. "Shower then," I said as I peeled off my damp shirt and let it drop on the floor, along with the rest of my clothes, on the way to the bathroom.

Like all of the studio cabins, I had a sweet bathroom, which had a massive tub and a marble tiled shower with enough room for two people. There was an overhead rain shower and jets along the walls. I stuck my hand in to check the water. I sure as hell didn't need to step into a lukewarm shower right now. I was aiming for steaming hot.

I heard a squeak and glanced over my shoulder to see Dani standing in the doorway, with all of the clothes I'd left behind in her arms. "I was just putting these in the hamper," she said hurriedly. She all but flung them into the hamper right inside the door.

"Nothing you haven't seen before," I drawled. "You can join me if you'd like."

My girl crossed her arms and shook her head. "You need to get warmed up. I'll make some hot cocoa." She scurried away.

With the water finally hot, I climbed in, calling in the direction of the door, "Are you planning to let me know what the hell you're doing here?"

I savored the hot water pounding down on me. Most nights when I came home like this, I would linger in the shower. I had no reason not to. Tonight, however, once I was warm all the way through, I stepped out.

Curiosity was simmering. Moments later, after scrubbing my hair dry with a towel, I glanced up to see Dani had been in while I was showering. A pair of sweatpants and a T-shirt, along with boxer briefs and socks, were sitting on the shelf above where the towels were.

I silently chuckled to myself. For crying out loud. I didn't need socks, and I sure as hell didn't need boxers, but Dani left them out for me, so I definitely put them on. Once my sweatpants and T-shirt were on, I headed into the main room of the studio-style cabin. I found Dani opening the small oven.

"Damn, it smells good in here. Whatcha making?" I slipped into a chair at the small round table.

Dani closed the oven and turned quickly to fetch a mug sitting on the counter beside the stove. She set it down in front of me. "Hot cocoa with that marshmallow vodka you like. I'm not actually making anything. I brought over some of that leftover potato leek casserole you like. I made it for lunch today for the staff. When I heard you guys had to go out in this awful weather, I figured you could use something warm when you got home."

She was standing at the counter, an oven mitt in one hand and her other hand twirling a lock of her hair that had fallen loose around her fingers. Her foot was tapping lightly on the floor.

Dani was nervous. I badly wanted to push. With her showing up uninvited and unannounced in my cabin after three days of hardly talking to me, I was a little bit confused. Not to cast too much blame in that regard. The last few days had been so packed, I practically had to schedule time to breathe and eat.

"Well, thank you. Of course I'm starving," I finally replied, before pausing to take a sip of the hot cocoa. It was fucking perfect. Dani's hot cocoa was a special kind of heaven. That marshmallow vodka was out of this world with it. It slid nice and smooth down my throat. After a few swallows, I leaned back in my chair and sighed, closing my eyes with a groan. Opening them again, I said, "Fucking delicious. Sit down. You're making me nervous just looking at you."

Her hand stopped twirling her hair. "I'm making you nervous?" she squeaked.

"Uh-huh," I drawled. "Stand if you like. How long until the food is ready?"

Dani glanced at the clock mounted above the stove. "Two minutes."

"Maybe you should have something to drink." I gestured to the mug sitting on the counter.

Dani's hand dropped from her hair before she lifted the mug and took a gulp. I followed suit, my eyes on her the entire time. Damn. I didn't think I'd ever get enough of looking at her.

And now, old memories that had faded around the edges were sharp and clear. I knew exactly how she felt against me. I knew the soft sounds she made. I knew how strong she was. I never did understand men who wanted a docile, polite woman. They didn't know what the hell they were missing.

Dani had a temper. Not a nasty temper, but a passionate

one. Everything with her was fierce—the good, and the bad. Her loyalty.

"Are you warm now?" she asked as she set her mug down.

"Yup. The hot shower took care of that."

Dani nodded, turning away to check the oven again before turning it off.

She was strung tight. I could feel the tension emanating from across the room. Seeing as I had already pushed my point days ago, I decided to stay quiet. She had yet to answer why the hell she was here, but I could wait. I was also starving, and my body's need for food overrode just about everything else.

When Dani set down a bowl of the casserole in front of me, my stomach let out a hearty growl and I gave over my focus. I had to admit it was awesome to come home tired, cold, and wet, and have Dani here to fuss over me and make me dinner.

I knew she would argue the point that she hadn't made *me* dinner, specifically. But Dani's cooking was divine. Her leftovers were good enough to be served in five-star restaurants as far as I was concerned.

We ate quietly. Once the edge was knocked off my hunger, I let the sense of comfort in this moment wash over me. Before I had crushed so hard on Dani back in high school, we'd been friends. I missed just hanging out with her. In the lead-up to those hot and heavy make out sessions we had in high school, we'd gotten closer and closer. She used to be the person I turned to for just about anything. Then, she broke my heart, or at least I thought she had.

A shaft of regret sliced through me. Not regret for anything I'd done, specifically, or Dani, for that matter. Rather, regret for life and the cards it sometimes dealt.

Dani stood, glancing over her shoulder to ask, "Do you want me to put the dishes in the dishwasher?"

"Sure thing. I just wait until it's full and then run it," I offered. "You don't have to clean up though."

Dani's eyes caught mine as she looked my way. Her gaze was pointed.

"I know, I know. You'd die before you left the kitchen messy," I teased as I stood up with my empty bowl.

I set the bowl in the rack beside hers as she rinsed the silverware before putting it in the small basket. When she closed the dishwasher and turned, I rested my hands on beside her hips on the counter.

"Okay, Dani girl, how about you tell me why you're spoiling me tonight?"

When I met her eyes, I saw uncertainty flicker for just a moment. But she lifted her chin slightly, that pretty pink blooming on her cheeks.

"I thought about what you said. I'm here."

I felt a flash—of wanting to tease Dani—but the moment she spoke, it passed. My heart kick-started in my chest. I might know what I wanted, or rather *who* I wanted, but I'd spent a few years being angry and confused with Dani. Then, a few more years attempting to tolerate her prickly boundaries.

I couldn't quite believe she wasn't swatting me away with some cutting remark. So, I held my tongue. After a moment, I felt her palm land in the center of my chest. There wasn't much distance between us, what with me caging her in between my arms. Those inches felt electrified.

Her hand broke through the barrier. Although her touch was light, I felt the reverberation of it through every cell in my body. Her eyes had fallen down, her thick lashes sweeping against her cheeks. They lifted again, questions swirling in them. "You're not gonna say anything?"

I sensed she wanted me to ease her anxiety. I could see the rapid flutter of her pulse at her throat and hear her short breaths. Stepping closer, I uncurled one hand from the counter and lifted it to pull out the pencil stuck in the bun on top of her head. Her hair fell in a messy tumble around her shoulders as I set the pencil on the counter behind her.

"There," I said gruffly. "I love your curls." I brushed them away from her face, one hand sliding over her shoulder and down her spine as I brought her body flush against mine.

"That's what you're saying?" Her voice was high-pitched with a slightly panicked edge to it.

"Oh, baby, we can't talk this one through. I told you how I felt. And you just told me that you're here. If there's one thing I know about you, it's that you're one of the strongest women I know. You sure as hell don't need me. So, if you're here, it's because you want to be. I also know, no matter how cliché it sounds, that actions speak louder than words."

"Words help things along," she muttered as I dusted a kiss on her temple and another right behind her ear.

"That they do, but I'm not so much in the mood for talking right now," I murmured, feeling the goose bumps forming on her skin as I made my way across. She shivered lightly in my arms. "You cold?"

She let out a little sigh. "I'm not cold."

"I sure hope not," I said as I cupped her sweet bottom and rocked my arousal into the cradle of her hips.

"What if...?" Her question ended with a little whimper when I nipped lightly at the juncture of her neck and shoulder in that sweet spot that I knew got her all worked up.

"Life is nothing but one giant 'what if,' darlin'," I said as I lifted my head, answering her incomplete question. "What if this is the exact right thing for us?"

Dani's eyes widened, and she bit her lip. "Lots of things have gone wrong for us."

"I know. We can't really screw it up any worse by seeing where things go now."

She held my gaze for a long moment before nodding. She was a worrier, always had been. I could only imagine that habit had been reinforced far more than was ever necessary by what went down that summer, years ago.

Since I knew I couldn't talk her out of worrying, I decided not to try. She was here, she was warm and curvy, and maybe mine. Christmas was only weeks away, and I'd give just about anything to know she was mine.

Bending low, I finally fit my mouth over hers. I had all kinds of ideas about taking things slow. There was one small problem with that idea. The moment our lips collided, it was pure combustion. The two of us together were fuel to the fire.

She opened her mouth for me immediately. With a little hitch in her throat and a little moan as she gasped into our kiss, I was *gone*. I growled in return as our tongues tangled. Squeezing her bottom once more and savoring the way her generous flesh gave under my fingers, I grabbed her hips with both hands and lifted her up on the counter. I needed access. Right quick.

Dani's legs curled around my hips, tugging me to her the moment I set her bottom down on the counter. Fuck. She felt so damn good. All soft and warm, smelling like cinnamon and sugar. I was a simple man. I didn't need fancy perfume or expensive clothes.

I just needed Dani.

Her hands slipped under my shirt, one sliding up my chest and the other gripping my back. She rocked her hips against the achingly hard length of my cock. My control was on a hair trigger, barely in check.

With a low growl, I broke from our kiss, gasping, "Dani. You're going to push me too fast."

She giggled, the sound so damn sweet, my heart squeezed tight. Only Dani elicited this familiar combination of raw, fierce lust undergirded by an intense yearning. That yearning was a combination of emotional and physical need, and the sweet, sweet joy of remembering what it felt like to be with this girl.

I knew she was all woman. Yet, she'd always be my girl.

"I don't know if we can go too fast," she said, her voice husky.

Leaning back slightly, I loosened my hand from where it had ended up tangled in her hair, sliding it over to cup her cheek. "Maybe not, but I don't want to miss a second. You're worth so much more to me than just a quick fuck."

Dani's breath came in a little startled huff as her eyes widened slightly. For just a second, I thought she might cry.

"Hey, what's that look for?"

She swallowed, and I sensed she wanted to look away. But she didn't. "It's just a lot. You know?"

"Is this your way of telling me things are complicated?" I asked, partly serious, and partly attempting to lighten the moment.

She wrinkled her nose, shrugging lightly. "Well, I mean, things *are* complicated. Not that it's anyone's fault."

"Baby, all that matters right now is you and me. Plus, I think you have too many clothes on."

She nudged her shoulder against my chest. "Then, I guess you better do something about that."

I didn't mind one bit being told what to do. Not by Dani.

"You tell me what to do and I'll do it. Let's get these clothes off."

Stepping back slightly, I hooked my hand in the hem of her shirt. She got right with the program, tugging it up and over her head and flinging it to the side. Nudging me back lightly with her knee, she shimmied off the counter.

"This is not a one-way street," she said pointedly as she eyed me with her hands on her hips.

With a grin, I stepped back. Our clothes came off in a tangle. Dani left hers in a trail behind her as she approached the bed.

When she turned to glance over her shoulder, by which point she had nothing on but a pair of bright purple cotton underwear, a hot bolt of lust slammed through me. .

"Hold up," I rasped. Dani stopped with her thumbs hooked over the edge of her panties. Her eyes met mine. "Let me help with that."

Shoving my boxers down, I ignored the throbbing pressure of my arousal as I closed the distance between us. Stopping in front of her, I trailed the backs of my fingers along the sweet curve of her hip, and into the dip of her waist before tracing them under the soft curves of each breast. Her nipples tightened, dusky pink in the dim light cast from the lamps in the corners.

I heard the soft hiss of her breath as I brushed back and forth over a nipple with my thumb before dipping my head down to drag my tongue around it.

"Turn around," I murmured.

She didn't hesitate, turning in my arms as I pressed hot, open-mouthed kisses along her neck while brushing her curls out of the way. She shivered in my arms as I let my hands play, teasing her breasts, mapping over the soft curve of her belly and cupping her mound with my palm. I felt the damp cotton before I hooked my thumbs into her panties and dragged them down over her hips.

"Mmmm." Her bottom pressed back against my cock. I teased my fingers between her thighs again, gratified to find her soaked, slick with the juices of her arousal. "Lean over," I ordered, my voice a husky growl.

With the bed in front of her, she obeyed immediately, resting her elbows on the mattress. I kneeled behind her, breathing in the scent of her as I nearly came just from the sight of her pink, glistening pussy.

"Wade," she gasped, her tone pleading.

I didn't mind admitting that turning Dani Love into a needy girl was a special thing. Sliding two fingers in her, I asked, "Yeah, baby?"

"I need—" Her words ended in a sharp cry when I leaned forward and dragged my tongue through her folds, swirling it around her clit.

I wanted this to take forever. But, dear God, when she begged, well, I couldn't deny her.

In a hot second, I was standing behind her. I took a moment to slide my cock back and forth through her slick arousal, a ragged groan escaping at the feel of it.

"So fucking ready. Just for me."

Dani's reply was indecipherable. Much as I could've come just from sinking inside of her right then, I needed to see her face.

Spinning her around, I stretched out beside her on the mattress. She shifted back on the pillows, beckoning me with her hands. "Hang on," I said.

In a flash, I snatched a condom out of the drawer beside my bed and rolled it on. Then, I was clasping her hands in mine and stretching her arms up over her head as my weight settled into the cradle of her hips.

Watching her, I released one of her hands and brushed her tangled curls away from her face. Dani was so guarded, so protected, and so fucking strong, it was breathtaking when her guard came down. Her cheeks were flushed and her eyes were wide open. Intimacy curled around us like smoke.

"Wade," she gasped, her hips rocking against me, her slippery core teasing my cockhead. With her dark green gaze pleading, I simply gave her what we both wanted.

My eyes on hers the entire time, I adjusted the angle of my hips and sank into her slowly, letting out a low growl. With her silken channel snug around my cock, I had to hold still to keep from coming right away.

When I met her eyes, my heart thudded so hard, the beat echoed through my entire body.

"This is exactly where we're supposed to be," I murmured before dipping my head and catching her lips in a kiss.

Chapter Twenty-One

DANI

This is exactly where we're supposed to be.

Wade's words echoed inside as he drew back and filled me again, the stretch decadent. I was entirely overwhelmed with sensation at the feel of him inside of me and all of him surrounding me.

Unlike the last time, I had approached tonight with my eyes wide open. My heart felt raw, exposed in a way I had never experienced. With pure physical need coursing through me, and Wade drawing back to sink inside of me again, sensation swept me into its current, each roll of his hips another wave crashing over me. Again and again, pleasure spun tighter and tighter in my core.

He lifted his head, murmuring something. I had no idea what he said, but I felt his intent in my heart and in his tone. When I dragged my eyes open, to see him above me, his dark, wide eyes on mine and his skin damp with sweat, I could hardly bear it.

One of his hands gripped mine tightly and the other cupped my cheek as he drove into me again, saying, "Give it to me."

I gave him everything, letting go on such a pure level that my orgasm left me breathless as the pleasure crashed through me. I distantly heard him cry my name and felt his cock pulsing inside of me as ripples of pleasure reverberated inside.

Wade fell against me, shifting instantly so his weight rested to the side. I didn't want him to move away so I hooked my leg tightly around his, murmuring into his neck, "Don't go anywhere."

In between a few heaving breaths, he chuckled. "Baby, I'm right here. Not going anywhere."

We didn't sleep much that night. We eventually untangled ourselves, and Wade pulled me into the bathroom with him. After he disposed of his condom and teased me to another climax with his fingers in the shower, we stumbled back to bed.

In chronological hours, I didn't sleep much. However, my rest was deeper than it had been since I could recall. We woke several more times, hands and lips exploring in the sleepy darkness. Wade was solicitous about condoms, using them two more times during the night. Perhaps more than most, that mattered to me. After the last time, I murmured, "I have an IUD."

Chapter Twenty-Two

WADE

"Eeeeeeek!"

At the wild screech, I turned to find a little boy barreling through the pasture. Without a blink, I took off at a run, far more relieved than I could imagine that my legs were easily twice as long as those belonging to the little boy.

Catching up to him in a matter of seconds, I swung him up in my arms and planted him on my shoulders before he had a chance to realize what was happening.

"Wow! How'd you do that?" the sandy-haired boy asked.

With my palms resting over his knees as I turned and headed back toward the barn, I replied, "It's my superpower."

He giggled.

"So that might've been funny, but I think you forgot the rules."

"What rules?" he chirped. His small hands held onto my forearms as I reached the gate, opening it and walking through to return to the where the rest of the first-grade class from Stolen Hearts Valley Elementary was waiting.

"Stay with your group. At all times. Most of the animals

here are friendly, but you never know what they might do when something unexpected happens," I explained.

"I just want to pet the horses," the little boy was saying as we reached his teacher's side.

The teacher glanced up, her eyes twinkling, although her expression was carefully controlled. I imagined this kid was a handful in the classroom. "Brian, you need to stay with the group. We're about to go meet the goats and the pigs," she said.

"Mr. Wade caught me. I promise I'll stay now," the little boy said as I lifted him over my shoulders and set him carefully on the ground.

"You will definitely stay because you'll be holding my hand for the rest of our tour," the teacher said with a smile.

I cast her a grin and turned to glance at Dawson. "What'd I miss?"

"Oh, nothing major. Let's head on into the rescue barn," Dawson replied with an easy smile. Usually, Jackson and I handled any tours that involved children, but Jackson was tied up with an emergency surgery at the vet clinic.

Dawson was generally a good sport, so I'd gone to fetch him. I considered handling it myself, but there were twenty kids here, just enough that we needed more eyes on them.

"Lead the way," Dawson said, gesturing toward the door of the rescue barn.

Looking to the group, I called, "All right, kids, follow me."

We tromped along a path, with a few kids bouncing in and out of the line, toward the rescue barn. Opening the barn doors, I entered first. We were immediately greeted by Gloria, the massive pig who'd become a bit of a mascot for the lodge as well as the rescue program. Gloria meandered over to the children. She ended up at the rescue program after a family who'd gotten her as a mini pig discovered she wasn't so mini. She was several hundred pounds now and friendly as ever. We usually didn't even keep her in the barn, and she wandered around the lodge at will. However, when we had groups like this, we wanted to make sure they got to meet her.

She snuffled and nudged the children, saying her version of "hello" to everyone. Of course, the kids loved her. Her much smaller companion, Squeaky, came from the side where they shared a stall. Squeaky was, in fact, a mini pig. Cute and nosy, she squeaked a lot. Hence, her name.

The kids fawned over her, and we went on to introduce the group to the goats and rescue dogs. Our next stop was back outside the barn where they could meet the chickens. The tour ended over at the horse barn in the lower level of the vet clinic where the little boy who had run into the pasture would get his chance to meet a few of the horses.

Shay usually helped with this part, but she had enlisted Dani to handle it because she was upstairs in the vet clinic managing the reception desk since the vet tech was working with Jackson. It had been several days since my night with Dani, and I'd been chomping at the bit to push things along. Hell, I wanted to skip past all the preliminaries and get right to the point. We were meant to be together, and I knew it.

But, she'd gone all prickly and guarded again, so I was biding my time. Considering my insane schedule, I was distracted enough to manage my impatience without much difficulty. With the Christmas holiday barreling toward us, the lodge was full. For one reason or another, our first responder team stayed busy with various emergencies.

Dani turned when we came through the main doors to the horse barn. Her brown hair was up in a messy ponytail with a pencil stuck through it, and I wanted to walk right up to her, yank that pencil out, and bury my hand in her curls while I kissed her. Needless to say, now wasn't quite the time for that.

The barn was nice and warm. The children walked down the aisle between the two rows of stalls.

"Hey, kids," Dawson said, stopping in the center of the aisle. "Let's wait for Dani to introduce all the horses."

Dani smiled, drawing my attention to her generous mouth. When she caught my eye, her cheeks pinkened slightly, and I had to tear my gaze away. Now definitely wasn't the time for me to tease, much less to think about just how much I'd been yearning for her.

"Okay, kids, I brought the horses in just to meet y'all. Let's start with Mischief, right over here," she began, gesturing to a pony who promptly stuck his head over his stall door at the sight of the children.

After Dani explained how Mischief came to be at the rescue program, a little girl's hand shot up. "Yes?" Dani asked, pointing toward her.

"How come Mischief doesn't get to go home, back to the Outer Banks?" the little girl asked.

"For the most part, the people in charge try not to interfere at all with the wild horses on the Outer Banks. But every so often, things happen. They were worried Mischief and his mother were going to die after he was born, so they took steps to take care of them. But once a horse has been rescued and domesticated, they can't let them back out in the wild. I promise Mischief is living the good life here," Dani explained.

The little girl nodded slowly, and Dani moved on, introducing the kids to the horses, one by one. Meanwhile, Dawson and I kept corralling the kids as a few of them darted in and out of the group.

After the teacher left with the kids, Dawson glanced my way. "Thank fucking God I didn't have to do this alone," he said bluntly.

"Oh yeah?" I drawled.

"Dude, I have *not* spent much time around kids. They kinda scare me."

I chuckled. "That mean you and Evie aren't planning on havin' any kids?"

A slight look of panic crossed Dawson's face. "I dunno. I'd never say no, but God only knows how I'll manage it."

Dani came out of the tack room where she'd gone to hang up the leads and halters. She glanced Dawson's way, fighting a smile. "Dawson, you're big enough to manhandle all of them at that age. I can't believe you're that scared of them," she teased as she leaned against the stall by Mischief. When he hung his head over the stall door, she idly reached over to scratch behind his ears.

Dawson shrugged easily. "Maybe so, but I guess I just have to get used to them. I didn't get much time with kids growing up like Wade."

I grinned. "It helps that my mom ran a daycare when I was a kid, so I was around them all the damn time. I love 'em," I said with a chuckle, just as our emergency phones went off.

Slipping my phone out, I glanced down. "Are you on duty today?" I asked, looking back over at Dawson.

"Sure am. Let's go," he said quickly.

When I looked toward Dani, her expression was tense. Something was spinning through her mind, and I wanted to know what. But, once again, time was not on my side. Duty called.

Chapter Twenty-Three

DANI

I sat on the examining table at my doctor's office. The thin paper crinkled with every tiny motion I made. The room was chilly, and I wondered why the office was never warm.

Looking down, I watched my feet swing back and forth, idly noticing my bright blue socks didn't quite match. For some random reason, one of them had faded more. Wiggling my toes, I kept swinging my feet. I was nervous and restless, and I had nothing else to distract me. There was a soft knock at the door, and I called, "Come in!"

The door opened and shut, and my doctor's face appeared as she pushed back the curtain encircling the corner where the door was. "Hi, Dani," Dr. Sue said with a smile as she glanced down at the computer tablet she held in her hands.

I'd been seeing Dr. Sue for my annual appointments since I was a teenager, so she knew me well. She had a warm smile and a round face, with twinkling brown eyes. She adjusted her glasses on her nose and looked up at me.

"You know, your glasses almost perfectly match your hair," I commented.

Her hair was a rich shade of brown and she had it pulled back into a bun. She stopped beside the table, the paper crinkling a little when she rested her hand on the edge. "Well, I'm glad to know something matches," she offered with a wide smile. "Seeing as I have to wear these most days"—she fingered the edge of her white lab coat—"I don't worry too much about matching. So, we're here for the usual, right?"

"Yep."

"All right then." She slipped her hips onto a rolling chair that had a small rotating tray mounted on the side for a laptop. She tapped on her tablet screen. "Okay, let's do the rundown."

She quickly ran through all the usual questions. At the end, she glanced up and asked, "Anything you're concerned about that I should know?" Fortunately, or unfortunately, she knew me well enough to see the hesitation in my gaze. "Go ahead and ask. I can't help you if you don't let me know what's going on."

I took a measured breath, trying to quell the anxiety rising inside. "Remember way back when that whole thing happened?" I was relieved I didn't have to explain the entire incident. She had been the doctor on call the night my mother brought me into the hospital. When she nodded, I continued, "You mentioned that because I had one ectopic pregnancy, there was a chance I might experience another."

Dr. Sue nodded slowly. "I did. Are you thinking about getting pregnant?"

I closed my eyes, willing the hot tears suddenly stinging to go away. After a moment, I thought I had it in hand and opened my eyes again. Dr. Sue also knew me well enough to wait me out.

"Not specifically right now, but I guess I'm wondering if it's the kind of thing I need to be careful about. Like, how great are the chances?" I finally asked.

Dr. Sue stood from her chair, stepping closer to lean her

hip against the side of the table and reach for one of my hands. It was ice-cold, which I hadn't even noticed until her warm hand closed around it. "God, it's freezing in here," she said with a brief shake of her head. "Please don't start researching online because that's a disaster. You can find any number of trails to follow that will terrify you."

A small laugh escaped. "I have actually refrained from doing so out of fear."

"We don't think about it very often, not since the era of modern medicine, but pregnancy is fraught with potential complications for any woman. It's true that once you've had one ectopic pregnancy, the data tells us you're at greater risk of having another one. More so than a woman who never had one. But, there are so many other things you could start worrying about, none of which are worth it. If you decide to get pregnant, I know your history, and we will monitor you carefully every step of the way. Many, many women who have ectopic pregnancies go on to have healthy pregnancies. Rather than focusing on the negative, let's focus on the positive."

I chewed the inside of my cheek as my feet started swinging again. I wanted a guarantee. I knew intellectually that wasn't possible for anything in life, but it didn't change what my heart wished for.

I finally nodded. "Okay." I didn't know what else to say.

She gave my hand another squeeze before stepping away to wash her hands quickly in a small stainless-steel sink in the counter running along the wall. She donned a pair of latex gloves and fetched the speculum.

"You ready?" she asked.

"I think you forgot to tell me to scoot my butt to the edge of the table and put my feet in the stirrups," I deadpanned.

Dr. Sue smiled. "That's because I'm confident you know the drill."

"Doesn't every woman?" I replied with a chuckle as I did just that.

While Dr. Sue quickly and efficiently did my annual exam, she continued talking. "I feel like I missed some news in your life. I saw your mom for her annual just last month, and she didn't mention anything about you being serious with anyone."

Even though I was lying on my back at this point with my hands folded over my stomach, my cheeks got hot. Blessedly, Dr. Sue was pulling off her gloves and washing her hands at the sink, so she couldn't see my face. There were many things I loved about living in a small town, but sharing a doctor with my mother wasn't one of them.

"I don't tell my mother everything, you know," I replied as I sat up.

Dr. Sue glanced over her shoulder while she dried her hands. "Well, I wouldn't expect that. I was just asking. Don't mean to be nosy. I've known you for so long, sometimes I get relaxed."

"Oh, it's okay. I don't mind you asking, and I wouldn't mind my mother asking. I guess I might be thinking about the possibility of something serious, and that got me wondering about things. Plus, turning thirty isn't too far off. Rumor has it my biological clock will start ticking so loud I might lose my hearing," I teased.

Dr. Sue laughed. "For some people, it does. But not everyone. I'm a fan of choice. If you decide you want to have children, that's a wonderful and amazing blessing. If you decide you don't, it's a wonderful and an amazing blessing to have it be your decision."

The paper tore slightly under my hips as I wiggled to the edge of the table. "I'm all about choices too. I don't know what I want just yet, but I suspect I might want to have kids. We'll see."

Chapter Twenty-Four

DANI

"Right this way," I said with a smile as I turned, menus in hand, and led a family through the restaurant to a table over in the corner. Setting the menus down, I waited until everyone was seated before speaking again. While I filled water glasses, I carried on my usual commentary. "If you already know what you'd like to drink, please let me know and I'll make sure your waitress gets it as soon as she can. Meanwhile, our specials tonight are ..."

I could reel the specials menu off without even thinking too hard. Considering I was the one who came up with the weekly specials, it was helpful my memory stayed sharp.

"Hey! Give me that!" the teen girl exclaimed as her eyes cut toward one of her twin brothers who had just snatched the menu out of her hands.

"Hey, buddy," the father said, his tone entirely unruffled and calm. "Give that back to your sister. Let's look at my menu together."

Immediately on the heels of the father settling down that minor kerfuffle, the other twin let out a screech. "Ow, he kicked me!" the little boy exclaimed, narrowing his brown eyes at his brother, who looked exactly like him, across the table.

This time, it was the mother who jumped in. "Remember, inside voices, please." She looked over to the boy I presumed to be the alleged kicker.

Without a word from her, he blurted out, "I didn't mean to. I was just wiggling in my chair."

"And what do you say? Even when it's an accident," the father said as he took a sip from the water I had just filled.

"Sorry," the boy said slowly.

The other boy looked mollified. When his mother ran her hand down his back and encouraged him to take a look at the menu, everyone moved on.

After I jotted down the requested glass of wine for the mother, a scotch for the father, the root beer for the teenager, and two glasses of apple juice for the kids, I hurried toward the bar.

"Apple juice?" the bartender, Griffin, asked as he glanced up.

"That's right. Two apple juices. It's for the kids. Evie has that table, so she'll be over to get the drinks in just a few, I'm sure," I said over my shoulder as I hurried away.

Pushing through the wide swinging door into the kitchen, I paused to hold it open for Evie. "By the way, I already got the drink order for the family I seated at table seven. Need help with that tray?" I asked as she adjusted the large tray resting on her shoulder and completely filled with plates.

"I got it," she replied with a smile as she turned, her brown ponytail swinging behind her while she hurried across the restaurant. Evie was one of my most solid waitresses. Always willing to pitch in and help, she was fast and efficient.

Out of habit, I scanned the line cooks. I tried to keep my kitchen running smoothly at all times, and we had a bumpy month or two before Thanksgiving, which had worried me.

Now though, the new staff we'd hired seemed to be settling into a rhythm with the rest of the team. With a satisfied nod to myself, I turned and headed out to the reception area. My mind lingered on the family I'd just seated. Although they clearly had their hands full with a set of twins, who looked to be around four or five, along with an older preteen, the parents were easygoing and both took a hand in responding to the kids in the middle of getting settled at a table at a restaurant. Having run a restaurant for years and working in them even longer all through college, I knew quite well that restaurants could be kryptonite for families with children.

Wade would be that kind of father.

Riiiight. Just what I need. To be thinking about what kind of father Wade would be.

I forcibly shoved him out of my thoughts and walked briskly to the front of the restaurant, practically having to chant "Don't think about Wade" in my mind.

I was relieved to find a line of customers stacked to the door when I rounded the corner. *Perfect. I need to be too busy to think.*

This was in contrast to late last night when I had been unable to sleep and found myself doing Internet searches about ectopic pregnancies and chances of future ones— entirely against the advice of Dr. Sue.

Conveniently, I stayed so busy this evening, I was about ready to collapse by the time we saw the last customer out the door. The holiday season kept us very busy. The Blue Ridge Mountains had pockets of cute towns and restaurants, and Stolen Hearts Valley happened to be one of the more popular areas. There was a ski resort about a half an hour away, so we got the overflow from them, in addition to all the customers at the lodge because Jackson found ways to keep us busy all year long.

Pausing after I locked the doors to the entrance, I glanced around, my eyes scanning the holiday decorations. I walked over and straightened one of the wreaths hanging on the wall that had likely gotten nudged out of place by someone's shoulder.

"Hey, I was just wondering where you were."

I followed the sound of Shay's voice to find her leaning in the archway that led into the main room of the restaurant. She held a bottle of wine in her hand.

"Well you found me. Are we having an after-work drink?" I asked with a tired smile.

"Yes. Evie texted me and told me it was nuts here tonight and that you had to call in Valentina for backup. Meanwhile, I was up to my eyeballs working on some website updates. I figured we could all use a few minutes to relax and unwind. You up for that?" she asked with a smile.

"Of course." Flicking off the lights, I fell into step beside her. We walked through the now empty restaurant. My eyes traveled over to the windows where the snow-tipped mountain ridge across the valley glowed a silvery white under the moon.

I took a breath and let it out, trying to shake the sense of melancholy I'd been feeling the last few days. By virtue of my nutty work schedule and Wade's, I'd managed to successfully avoid another night with him. Part of me felt like that was an achievement, while another part of me longed for him so deeply, I felt it in my bones.

When we stepped into the kitchen, my heart jump-started at the sound of his laugh.

Shay happened to look over her shoulder at just that moment. She stopped abruptly. "Oh. Was I supposed to warn you the guys were here too?" she asked, sotto voce.

"No," I squeaked. "It's totally fine."

Steeling myself to withstand the sheer temptation of Wade's presence, I walked over toward the ovens. Knowing Evie, she probably already put in any leftovers to warm. Upon opening one of the ovens, I was pleased to see a loaf of garlic bread was already warm, in addition to a pan of arti-choke dip.

"Thanks, Evie! That all we got?" I called over to Evie as she strode toward me, sipping a glass of wine.

Reaching up, she took the elastic off of her ponytail, sending her glossy brown hair in a tumble around her shoul-ders. "That's it. Can you believe it? It'll have to do. Come sit down. I'll check on it in a few minutes," she said as she slipped her hand through my elbow and tugged me over toward the picnic-style table at the back of the staff kitchen.

Because I was that unlucky, Wade slid over immediately, opening up a spot at the end of the bench just as I reached the table. "Here, get her a glass of wine, Wade," Evie ordered. "I'm going to get the food and plates."

"No, you're not." Dawson stood abruptly. "You've been on your feet, waiting on tables all night. You're not waiting on us," he said with a smile as he dipped his head and pressed a kiss against the side of her neck.

Their intimacy was so casual and easy, it made my heart squeeze. Wade was pouring me a glass of wine, leaving me little option but to sit down beside him and enjoy it. Anything else, and it would seem like I was being difficult. As it was, I already knew most of our shared friends thought I had an attitude with him.

Even though I was loath to admit it, they were right. I was cultivating my casual attitude. Although, that was incredibly difficult. Especially given the fact that just having his fingers brush against mine as I sat down and accepted a glass of wine from him sent a hot sizzle of electricity spin-ning up my arm and radiating through my body.

"We were just voting on who had the longest day," Wade said with a slow grin.

Dear God. All he had to do was grin and my belly spun. I took a deep breath and a healthy gulp of my wine. "So, who's winning the vote?" I asked, hoping the flush suffusing my body wasn't obvious.

"So far," Shay said as she sat down across the table from me, "it's you."

"Me? All I know about the day is everybody in the restaurant was practically running a race just to keep up. And you guys," I said, casting my eyes across Wade, Jackson, and Walker, "always have crazy days."

"Yeah, but we figured you were the only one up making bread at five in the morning," Wade drawled from my side.

I chuckled. "Maybe so."

Just then, Dawson returned to the table, quickly passing out plates for everyone before striding back to the oven to pull out the garlic bread and artichoke dip.

Once he was seated again, I caught his eye and winked. "You know, if you ever need some extra cash and want to cover backup shifts ..."

Dawson threw his head back with a laugh. "I don't think so. I can handle this, but dealing with all those customers?" He gave a little shudder before reaching over to spoon some dip onto his plate.

Conversation meandered slowly as people sipped drinks and nibbled on our small fare for this late evening snack. *This* was what I loved about my job. Because it was more than a job. Working here felt like being part of a family.

When I felt Wade's big palm curl over my thigh and a hot jolt of need spun through me, I prayed that whatever we had unleashed didn't ruin us.

Walker, one of the newer of the group here, was asking Jackson just how busy things got in the summer.

Jackson ran a hand through his shaggy brown hair and cracked a grin. "Fucking busy, man."

Wade chimed in. "Oh yeah. You think we're busy now, wait until spring hits."

Dawson added, "Just hope you weren't lying when you said you enjoyed leading hikes. We're booked with those all summer long."

Walker flashed a smile. "Oh, I meant what I said about

that. I like to stay busy, and I love to be outside."

At that moment, there was a knock at the back door to the staff kitchen entrance. "Well, that's odd," I commented as I stood from the table.

"Yeah, who the hell knocks around here?" Dawson commented.

Striding to the door, I swung it open to find Lucas's sister, Jade, waiting there. "Oh, hey, Jade. What's up?"

A blast of cold winter air blew in as I held the door open. The sharp sting of sleet struck my cheeks with the wind. "Come on in," I said. "It's freezing out."

Jade stepped in with her arms wrapped tightly around her waist as she shivered slightly. "Oh, thank you." She shared her older brother's coloring, with her black hair and green eyes. She smoothed her damp hair with a hand.

"Is it sleeting out there?" I asked.

Jade sighed. "Something between snow and rain. Sorry to bug y'all, but I got a flat tire. I was driving home from Lost Deer Bar. I must've driven over a nail or something. I was hoping somebody might be headed in my direction, and I could catch a ride."

Shay called over from the table. "Why don't you stay a few minutes to warm up? Do you want something to eat or drink?"

Jade followed me to the table. "Oh, thank you. I'm not hungry at all. But I'll hitch a ride with whoever's going in my direction." She glanced at Jackson. "I hope it's okay I left my car at the end of the drive. I parked it in the little pullout near the sign."

"Of course it's okay. Your brother's not around. He already came and stole Valentina from us," Jackson teased.

"I know," Jade said. "He was the first person I called when my tire started feeling all wobbly."

Jackson glanced at Walker and asked, "Don't you live out on the west side of the valley?"

Jade looked toward Walker. "I don't think we've met,"

she said politely. "I'm Jade Cole. If you work here, you probably know my brother, Lucas. I live on Blue Creek Lane."

Walker stayed true to his typically quiet form and simply nodded before replying succinctly, "I live on the same road. Happy to give you a ride."

I bit back the urge to point out I wasn't sure Walker ever looked too happy. He had the whole tall, dark, and mysterious vibe going strong. But he'd only been here a month or so, so I didn't know him well enough yet to know if I could tease like that.

"That would be great," Jade replied quickly.

"Well, that's all settled then," I said as I rounded the table to fetch my almost empty glass of wine. I was relieved for Jade's interruption because it gave me a reason to create some physical distance between Wade and me.

Quickly draining my glass, I glanced around the table and started picking up the empty plates and glasses.

"Are we done?" Wade asked. There was a teasing glint in his eyes when I glanced down as I picked up his empty bottle of beer.

"I don't know if you're done, but I'm gonna clean up and go get some rest."

Walker stood at that moment, commenting, "I need to head out too. Thanks for the food and drinks."

Jade had turned away and was saying something to Shay. I didn't miss how Walker's gaze lingered on her. Jade was lovely—as beautiful as her brother was handsome. She had a strong cast to her features, bold cheekbones and nose, with dark brows. Until I'd gotten to know her, she'd intimidated me a bit.

I watched as Walker looked her up and down, his gaze inscrutable. I didn't miss his open curiosity though. Jade had declared herself permanently single, so I sent up a silent wish for Walker. If he wanted her, he was going to have to go all-out.

Within a few minutes, the group gradually broke up. I

actually savored the quiet time in the kitchen when everyone was gone. I puttered around, wiping down surfaces and checking on things. I set the last few plates in the dishwasher to run in the morning.

Turning, I jumped slightly when I found Wade standing by the doorway that led into the hallway where my office was. My hand flew to my chest. "I didn't realize you were here! You scared me."

Wade leaned his shoulder against the doorframe, with one hand hooked in the pocket of his jeans. God, he was so damn sexy with his brown hair and dark espresso eyes. I wanted to walk over and lean into him, letting his strength encompass me.

He was quiet for a few beats as he watched me walk toward him. "Just waiting. Figured I'd walk you home."

My heart was beating rapidly. I wanted to stop right where I was until I could get a grip. But it was going on midnight, and I was truly exhausted.

Stopping in front of him, his scent assailed me. A hint of the winter air clung to him. He must've walked outside since I started to busy myself in the kitchen.

Looking into his eyes, the words that strolled out shocked me. "Just so you know, once someone's had an ectopic pregnancy, there's a greater risk of having another one."

What the hell? Why are you bringing this up now?

Wade's eyes widened slightly. "Um, okay. Is there a reason you're mentioning this now?"

I tried to take a breath, but a sob caught in my throat. I so did *not* want to fall apart in front of Wade. I masked my sob by clearing my throat and shaking my head. When I could manage a breath, I replied, "I just thought you should know. I know how much you love kids."

Wade's dark eyes scanned my face. His mouth opened and closed. "Look, you're exhausted. Maybe we should save this conversation for another time. Let me walk you back."

Chapter Twenty-Five

WADE

To put it bluntly, the weather sucked. Icy rain fell from the sky, striking my cheeks with stinging cold. It was about a five-minute walk from the lodge restaurant along the path through the trees to Dani's cabin, but even I was shivering by the time we got there.

The holiday lights strung through the trees were blurred by the rain. Dani stumbled as she climbed up the two steps onto her porch. I caught her by the hip and shoulder. "Easy," I said, my voice nearly drowned out in the rain.

I could feel the tremors running through her body. "God, it's cold. I can't believe Jade walked all the way down the main drive in this rain," she replied.

"She needed a ride, so she was motivated," I said as I turned the knob and pushed her door open, holding it open while she stepped inside.

Following her in and not certain if I was welcome, I breathed a sigh of relief when I closed the door behind us, shutting out the wet cold.

"Damn, I didn't know the rain was going to roll in so

fast," I commented as I tossed the hood back on my rain jacket and shook it lightly.

Dani glanced up from toeing off her wet tennis shoes, her big green eyes bright with her spiky wet eyelashes framing them. "Me neither. When Shay came to get me after the restaurant closed, I could still see the moon over the mountains on the other side of the valley."

She hung her jacket on the hook by the door, not saying anything else. Meanwhile, I could practically hear the gears shifting in her brain. I was a patient man. I could wait her out. I certainly wasn't going to be pushy tonight, not after her comment earlier.

When I saw her shiver slightly, it tested my restraint and patience, because I wanted to lift her into my arms and carry her into the shower where we could both warm up. When she turned back to me, I saw the hesitation in her eyes. Much as I wanted to hold her tonight—because it had been too many days now—I called upon my discipline and pushed away from the door where I'd rested my shoulder.

"I'll go now. Make sure you get something warm to drink." I started to turn away, steeling myself to walk into the rain and leave Dani behind.

"Wade." The sound of my name in her frayed voice drew me back instantly, like a puppet on a string.

"Look," she began, pausing as she took a shaky breath. She caught one of her curls in her finger, spinning it in a circle and betraying her nervousness. "I guess maybe I kind of dumped that on you back there ..." Her words trailed off again as she gestured vaguely in the direction of the lodge.

"Dani," I said, shaking my head slightly. "You're freezing, I'm wet, and we're both tired. We can talk later."

While I didn't quite know why Dani felt the need to let me know she faced more risky odds than most women when it came to having children, it wasn't something I worried about. Having lost my own mother when I was too young to remember her, I understood far too well how life could deal an unfair hand.

Although I'd had no choice but to accept that loss, I also knew how lucky I was. My father remarried a few years after my mother died and before I even started kindergarten. The woman who became my stepmother went on to adopt me. She loved me fiercely and, to me, she was my mother in every way that mattered. It didn't matter to me, not one iota, whether or not she had carried me into this world.

Dani shivered again, wrapping her arms around her waist. "I know—" She gave her head a little shake this time, biting off whatever she was about to say. "Do you want some hot cocoa?" she asked abruptly.

I would take whatever Dani would give me so, of course, I said yes. A look of relief crossed her face. "Okay. Perfect. Get your shoes off and get out of that wet coat," she ordered.

If there was one thing that righted the ship of Dani, it was having something to do. Making sure someone had something hot to drink on a cold winter night was right up her alley. She also felt best when ordering people around.

Turning, I leaned over to unlace my boots. I kicked them off as I shrugged out of my wet jacket, more droplets of cold water falling to the floor as I hung it up.

"Want me to clean this up?" I asked, gesturing to the damp tile in the small entryway.

Dani rolled her eyes when I looked at her where she stood in the small kitchen area just across the room. "Isn't that why it's tiled?"

I chuckled and shrugged as I padded into her bathroom to fetch a towel. I quickly snagged a clean one off the shelf and scrubbed it over my damp hair.

"Need a towel?" I called through the doorway.

"No thanks. Unlike you, I actually zipped up my jacket."

Smiling to myself, I hung the towel on one of the hooks

on the back of the door and returned to the main room. Dani had milk heating on the stove and was shaving a chunk of dark chocolate with a knife.

"Oh, you're going old-school," I said as I slipped into a chair at the small round table.

She smiled, her gaze slightly bashful as she looked over at me. "Always. It's best this way."

The room fell quiet as she puttered at the stove. The day's tension unspooled inside while I let the feel of being in Dani's presence wash over me.

A few minutes later, she handed me a mug and set a bottle of my new favorite marshmallow vodka in the middle of the table. "This way, you can make it as strong as you like," she explained.

Although I had told her our conversation could wait, I could practically feel the words wanting to press out of her. When Dani had something on her mind, she wasn't much for waiting to get it out.

After a few sips and adding a liberal dash of vodka, I cocked my head to the side. "Baby, if you wanna talk, lay it on me."

She caught one of her curls again and started spinning it around her finger. Reaching over, I clasped her hand in mine. "I don't know what's got you so worked up, but just relax."

"I'm pretty sure there has *never* been a time in history when someone relaxed just because someone else told them to," she muttered, irritation flashing in her eyes.

Keeping a hold of her hand—because she didn't yank it away—I gave it a gentle squeeze. "I know, baby. I guess I should've said something along the lines of 'I hate seeing you worry, and I wish you wouldn't.'"

Her lips kicked up on one side. "I guess I already said everything I needed to say. I just thought it was something you should know."

"Because you had one ectopic pregnancy, you might have

another?" I asked before pausing to take a healthy sip of my cocoa.

She nodded. "Yeah. That's it."

"Okay," I said slowly. "I can't really tell if you're upset about that, or not."

She shrugged and took a gulp of her cocoa. I could feel her knee bouncing up and down under the table. She was anxious as all hell about this, but she wasn't giving me much to go on. Knowing there was no sense in me interpreting something until she was ready to explain, I gave her hand another squeeze. "I'll say it again. I'm sorry you basically had to go through that alone. It must've been scary as hell."

She bit her lip, pulling her hand out from under mine. "I'm okay. It was a long time ago."

I was a man, but I was no idiot. I sensed there were all kinds of undercurrents rippling under the surface here, including cross currents and crazy shit like that. Without knowing what was going on inside her busy brain, all I wanted was to somehow ease her anxiety.

"Darlin', you're a thinker. You always have been. You're smart as hell, so that's a good thing. But stop thinking so hard right now. You're worrying, and you're not telling me what you're worrying about, so I don't know how to help. I'm sorry to tell you, but my mind-reading abilities were always on the weak side."

Dani cracked a smile as she laughed softly. "Fair enough. I certainly don't expect you to read my mind. You're right, I tend to worry."

"Can we hit the pause button on it for now?"

She nodded, leaning forward to lift her mug again.

After we talked about nothing but the mundane and sipped her delectable cocoa for a bit, her head began drooping to her shoulder. I knew she would be getting up truly before the crack of dawn. Much as my body had an opinion—it always did when it came to Dani—I nudged her into bed and tugged the down comforter around us. I was beyond content, given how tired I was, to fall asleep with her warm in my arms. It had never been just about sex when it came to Dani.

Chapter Twenty-Six

DANI

"Thanks, Nancy," I said, taking the cup of coffee she handed over the counter to me.

Nancy flashed a distracted smile, already turning to greet a customer waiting behind me. Wake & Bake Café stayed busy all the time by virtue of its convenient location in downtown Stolen Hearts Valley. In spring, summer, and fall, it catered to the touristy groups passing through the Blue Ridge Mountains looking for a beautiful drive, or a few days vacation. Come winter, although there weren't as many travelers, the local traffic picked up the pace.

As far as I was concerned, there wasn't much better than a hot cup of coffee from Nancy, who owned Wake & Bake Café with her husband, Dan. Although I prided myself on making a mean cup of coffee for the staff and the customers at the lodge, I was always quick to recommend Wake & Bake Café to anyone simply looking for damn good coffee.

"Dani, dear," Nancy called as I turned away. Glancing back, I raised a brow. "Your bagel with cream cheese will be out in just a few minutes. My daughter will get it for you."

I gave her a thumbs-up and wove through the tables to

snag one by the front windows looking out over Main Street. The icy rain that had begun two nights ago and lasted through yesterday had finally turned to snow last night. It left our pretty little town nestled in the mountains covered with fairy dust.

The sun wasn't up yet, with merely the glimmers of its rays reaching above the mountain range on the far side of town. The early morning sky was stained pink with a silvery, lavender hue, casting a faint glow on the thin layer of snow covering the landscape. I took a sip of my coffee, letting out a sigh of approval as the rich, dark brew slid down my throat. Although I wasn't actually working in the restaurant this morning, I was still up early. I was so accustomed to getting up early, I figured I would, even if I had absolutely nothing to do. I found it quite doubtful there would ever be nothing to do in life.

"Hey, sweetheart," my mother's voice said from over my shoulder.

Looking to the side, I saw her hurrying my way, her giant purse weighting down one shoulder and another bulky bag dangling from her other arm. When she reached the table, my mother leaned over to press a kiss on my cheek before straightening and letting her bags slide off her arms.

"Morning, Mom. Need some help?"

I began to stand from my chair but my mother waved me away. "Don't you dare get up. I'm just gonna leave these bags before I get out of this giant coat and go get a coffee."

After she had done precisely that, she hurried over to the counter. She conferred for several minutes with Nancy before returning with her own cup of coffee and my bagel generously slathered with jalapeño cream cheese.

"Well, Nancy seems just fine. It's always good to catch up with her. I don't get in here enough, you know?" my mother said as she set the small plate with my bagel down in front of me. She sat down and immediately took a hearty gulp of her coffee.

I enjoyed a bite of my bagel while she got settled. After a moment, she brushed an errant curl out of her eyes. I had inherited my unruly brown curls from my mother. Hers were still wild, but they were now streaked with silver standing out amidst the brown. I had also inherited my round face and freckled cheeks from her. We shared the same build as well, curvy and on the short side.

Otherwise, my mother had a rather brash personality. I knew I could be brash, although I tended to think that side of me had been tampered by my rather strict father. My father had loved me, but he hadn't been the warm and fuzzy type.

My mother, on the other hand, was effusively warm and opinionated with everyone. Her tendency to speak her mind had tested my father's patience throughout the entirety of their marriage. However, he'd loved her, and I imagined he appreciated it anyway. That said, he certainly hadn't encouraged me to be as bold and brash as her.

"I'm so glad you escaped the kitchen for a morning," she finally said, leaning across the table to squeeze my hand. "I brought a bunch of treats for the animals in the rescue. That's what's in there." She gestured to the bag by her feet.

"I'm sure Jackson and Shay will appreciate that. How are you, Mom?"

"I am just fine, dear. Staying busy at the hospital, how about you?"

My mother was a nurse and worked an intense schedule at the hospital. I supposed I got my workaholic tendencies from her. "I'm doing fine. Always busy, but then, the restaurant never slows down."

My mother pursed her lips. "Working is all you're doing. I sure hope Jackson appreciates it. You are making him a ton of money," she huffed.

Although she would work herself to the bone for someone else, she tended to hover and worry about me. "Mom, he pays me really well, and I love my job."

"Of course. Jackson Stone is a good man and always has been. If he hadn't fallen in love with Shay, I might've tried to play matchmaker with y'all."

I almost choked on the bite of my bagel I had just taken. After I recovered, I leveled my mother with a glare. "Seriously, Mom? Don't you even start thinking about matchmaking me with anyone. Not to mention, I have never felt anything even remotely like that for Jackson. He's just a friend and nothing more."

My mother laughed. "Oh hon, I was teasing. I try to stay out of your business. If I was ever going to dedicate myself to matchmaking, I'd try to get you and Wade reunited."

With that casual comment, she left me speechless. The tips of my ears felt hot, and I knew my cheeks were red. I stuffed a bite of bagel in my mouth, needing something to keep me from freaking out in the middle of Wake & Bake Café.

I chewed rapidly and took another bite, feeling my mother's gaze on me the whole time. After I somewhat gathered myself together, I took a sip of coffee and brushed my curls off my shoulders. "What the hell are you thinking?" I asked bluntly.

"Hon, I was kind of teasing but serious at the same time. Your reaction lets me know I was spot on."

"Uh, no."

"Uh, yes. He's the only boy you ever really liked. You two were friends for a long time first. Then, that summer happened and that was it."

"Mom, do I need to remind you that Dad forbade me from even talking to Wade, much less seeing him again after everything went down?"

A look of sadness passed over my mother's face. "You don't need to remind me. I remember quite clearly. I wish I had done a better job of helping your father get a handle on that. It's no excuse, but he was terrified, so he tried to control the situation. That was a terrible idea. He never should have forbidden you from talking to Wade, and I'm so sorry he ever did."

I took a sip of coffee to try to push through the emotions bottling up tightly in my throat and chest. My mother, remarkably, stayed quiet. Although, I supposed it wasn't that remarkable.

Opinionated though she could be, she was a fiercely loyal mother and friend to anyone she cared about. She knew when to allow silence. In this case, she clearly sensed I needed a moment.

After another sip of coffee, the threat of tears had passed. "So, it wasn't just me?" I finally asked.

My mother shook her head slowly. "Definitely not. That's just how he dealt with things. His years in the military suited him perfectly. He lived to have a plan for everything. The flip side to that was not all of life is structured and orderly. There are too many unknown contingencies. He most certainly didn't know how to handle a teenage daughter who was a bit too much like me," she said with a rueful smile.

That brought a huff of a laugh from me. My chest loosened enough for me to take a deep breath and let it out slowly. "I don't guess I was easy for him." I thought of my father, whose routine was so predictable when he was alive, I could've set my clock by it. Looking to my mother, I added, "I always thought I got my early morning habits from him."

"Well you certainly didn't get that from me," she said with a sly grin before pausing to sip her coffee.

After another fortifying gulp of my own coffee, I forged into the no-go zone of conversation. "Did he ever talk much with you about what happened that summer?"

My mother nodded slowly. "He was the kind of man who needed time to process things. So, it took a while. At first, he was terrified. Like I said, he did what he could to try to control the situation. I should've talked with you sooner about this."

I lifted a shoulder in a small shrug. "It's not like I asked. It's a pretty heavy topic."

My mother's eyes searched my face, and I abruptly wished she didn't know me so well. "Of course it's a heavy topic. But I've always prided myself on not being one of those mothers who avoided the difficult issues. I'm realizing I avoided the most difficult one quite spectacularly. I guess I knew it hurt you, so I didn't want to rub salt in the wound, if you know what I mean. I think if there had been more time for your father, he would've eventually talked to you and admitted he overreacted. He was still upset with Wade, mind you. But then, I don't know how many fathers ever get comfortable with the idea of their daughter having sex with anyone."

A bitter laugh slipped out. My heart felt sore, like an old wound that never fully healed had been probed. It wasn't awful, and I could deal with it, but I knew it would always be there. I didn't suppose you could be seventeen years old, get pregnant by accident, and almost die from an ectopic pregnancy without it being something you carried with you forever.

"I wish we'd had a chance to talk," I finally said.

"It became the taboo subject, and then your father got sick. Speaking of things not being orderly, there's only so much planning you can do in life. I certainly didn't expect your father to die when he did. Heart attacks are sneaky thieves."

The pain in my mother's eyes lingered, and I knew she missed my father dearly. Despite my own mixed feelings about him, I knew my father had been a good man. He'd been flawed, just like everyone. I knew he and my mother had loved each other deeply. As different as they'd been, I'd always thought those differences bound them more tightly together and strengthened the love they had.

"I know you miss him. I do too. I don't have anyone to

call to fix my car anymore," I said, my lips lifting at the corners.

My mother's eyes brightened with her smile. "You could always ask Wade," she teased, smoothly shifting gears.

"Oh, I should've known that was coming," I muttered, casting her a mild glare.

"So tell me, what *is* going on with you and Wade?"

I took a breath and shrugged. "I'm not quite sure. For a long time, I avoided him. Now, I guess we're feeling our way through things."

"Whatever you do, don't let your stubbornness get in the way."

Chapter Twenty-Seven

DANI

"Daddy!" Rylie squealed as she ran across the kitchen and leapt in the direction of her father.

Lucas caught her easily, swinging her into his arms and smoothing her dark hair away from her face before pressing a kiss to her forehead. "Hey, sweet pea. How was your afternoon?"

"Good!" Rylie proceeded to reel off a list of everything she had done with me this afternoon. I had volunteered to let her hang out with me in the kitchen since Valentina had a deadline to meet with some accounting paperwork, while Jade had been tied up with some appointments and unable to babysit for the afternoon.

Lucas eased her down as Rylie continued chattering. "So, it sounds like you had fun," he commented once she paused to take a breath.

Clinging to his hand, Rylie nodded. "Dani can babysit anytime," she said with an earnest nod.

I dusted my hands on my apron before turning to wash them quickly in the sink across from the stainless-steel table where I'd been working with Rylie. "We had a great time together today. Rylie knows I'll be backup anytime," I offered with a wink as I turned back to face them.

"Thanks again," he said as Rylie broke away to meander over to pick up her cup of water and take several gulps.

Right then, the back door to the staff kitchen opened again. Wade stepped through, bringing a gust of chilly air with him as he closed the door. My heart did a little dance before taking off at a wild gallop.

Wade opened his mouth to say something but looked away when Rylie squealed his name and went dashing across the kitchen again. She spilled her water on the way over when she knocked her foot against the edge of the small stepladder. It had been serving as a shelf for her cup and various baking items, including the green and red sprinkles we'd used to decorate a batch of holiday cookies.

"Wade!" she repeated when she skidded to a stop in front of him.

Wade dropped one of his big hands on her thin shoulder. "Well, hey there, Miss Rylie. Looks like you spilled your water. Do you need some help cleaning it up?"

When Rylie's eyes widened, it was almost comical. "Oopsies. I made a mess. I can handle it," she said as she looked back toward the stepladder and the small splatter of water beside it.

With a warm smile, Wade nodded down at her, nudging her between her shoulder blades. "Why don't you go take care of it? I knew you could handle it yourself."

It was a testament to just how freaking bad I had it for Wade that watching this little interaction made me want to hand my ovaries over to him on the spot.

While Rylie gathered up too many paper towels to wipe up her water, Lucas and Wade approached me where I stood by the baking prep table.

"Please tell us you have some snacks," Wade said bluntly, the teasing glint in his eyes sending my belly into a tumbling routine, with a shivery feeling racing through my body.

"I always have snacks. With you boys usually coming by when you're starving, it's to my benefit to keep the complaints to a minimum," I replied.

Turning, I walked over to the oven mounted on the wall, opening it and sliding out a large pepperoni pizza. Pizza was an easy favorite, and I could leave the oven on warm and have it here for anyone who happened to pass through.

"This one was only ready about twenty minutes ago," I explained. "I've just been keeping it warm."

Wade let out a groan and snagged a stool to pull it by the table. I left the pizza on a tray and fetched plates, napkins, and silverware. He took a slice and bit into it before leaning back and closing his eyes with a satisfied sigh.

"Geez, man," Lucas murmured. "Don't forget you have a six-year-old audience."

Wade's eyes snapped open. "I'm just enjoying food," he mumbled in between bites.

Lucas chuckled. "Yeah, I know. Mind if I take some home?" he asked, his gaze cutting over to me.

"Of course not. I know you need to get home. It's already dark, and I'm sure you need a little time to get Rylie ready for bed."

"That I do. More than that, I need a shower," Lucas said.

Both men had muddy boots and looked tired. One of Wade's cheeks was decorated with a little dirt for good measure.

"I'll get you a take-home box," I said as I turned to do just that.

"Do I get a piece?" Rylie called as she ran back after putting her cup in the dishwasher rack and tossing the paper towels in the trash.

"I don't know. How much did you eat this afternoon?" Lucas asked.

"She just had a snack of peanut butter and apple slices. I've been mostly working on bread and holiday cookies.

Rylie was a big help," I explained as I returned to the table with a pizza box.

"Dani said she didn't want me to ruin dinner," Rylie said with a pleased smile

Lucas grinned. "All right then. One slice of pepperoni for you. Do you happen to know what time Valentina will finish up?" he asked.

"I do. She texted me to tell you when you came for Rylie to head over to the clinic. She said she just finished up, so she doesn't need to catch a ride with someone else later."

Rylie clapped her hands together. "Yay!"

Within a few moments, Lucas had a pizza box in hand and Rylie trailing behind him as they waved good night.

"Dani!" Evie called as she poked her head through the swinging door into the restaurant kitchen.

"You need me?" I returned, experiencing a shaft of disappointment. I had wanted some time alone with Wade. Because, yeah, I was a little crazy about him. Against my better judgment.

"Just for a sec," she replied quickly before swinging back into the front. The noise from the restaurant kitchen increased in volume and then muted as the door swung closed behind her.

Glancing to Wade, I said, "Be right back."

He was already picking up another piece of pizza and taking a bite, but he nodded. Hurrying to the front, I walked through the hustle and bustle of the kitchen, my eyes reflexively scanning the room. Everything appeared to be running smoothly, like the well-oiled machine I strove for when I was training staff.

Stepping from that organized chaos into the front area of the restaurant, I glanced around, wondering where Evie had gone. When I walked through the archway toward the reception desk, I saw the exact problem. Grace was handling hostess duties tonight and had one of my least favorite customers at the desk. John Burton was an asshole. A rich asshole. He was also older and cranky, and liked to come in and complain. I didn't even bother finding out what the specific issue was before striding to the desk.

"Hi, John, what can I do for you?" I asked, just as he repeated my name to Grace.

"Dani," he said, his bushy white eyebrows raised. "I know I made a reservation, but this young lady is telling me that you don't take reservations this time of year. I am *not* interested in waiting."

I smiled sweetly. "John, it's impossible for you to make a reservation because it's exactly as Grace explained. We're so busy during the holiday season that we do not take reservations. I'm sure you'd like to have your dinner right away, but you're going to have to wait."

"Dani, I'm not gonna keep bringing my business here," John said with a huff and a wag of his chubby finger in my face.

"I'm sorry to hear that, John. If that's the case, I'm sure you'll take your business somewhere else."

This was John's routine. Bully, pressure, and bully. I personally didn't care one iota if he chose never to come to our restaurant again. We had more than enough polite customers.

He stared at me, and I knew this was the point where he expected me, or whoever was on the other end of his cranky attitude, to cave. I held his gaze, and my ground.

"Fine then," he finally muttered. "We won't be eating here tonight." He marched out, his wife trailing behind him without so much as a glance in our direction. I couldn't even imagine being married to him.

As soon as he was gone, I said to Grace, "Don't ever worry about him. If you need me and I'm here, just come get me."

Grace looked slightly frazzled and was already fielding a request from someone else, so I squeezed her shoulder. "You got this?"

"Of course. Thanks for coming to deal with John."

I hurried to the back, relieved no one else intercepted me. When I pushed through the door into the staff kitchen, I came face to face with the recognition a tiny part of me had worried Wade would gobble up his pizza and leave. That shouldn't have been a big deal, but it sure felt like one.

When I came through the door and the busy sounds muted behind me, the *thud* of my heartbeat echoed in my ears as I crossed the kitchen to where he sat on the stool beside the table. Oblivious to my internal distress, he finished off a slice of pizza and flashed a crooked grin. "That was fucking delicious," he said bluntly.

His presence eased the anxiety spinning inside me, and I managed a breath. "I aim to please," I replied, unaccountably pleased with his comment. I did love to cook, and I was quite proud of the success of the restaurant. Yet, more than anything, it meant a lot to see that warm smile on his face. As I stood there, maybe two feet away, I felt caught in the beam of his gaze. That familiar fire that never died inside flared hot.

He reached out, catching my hand in his and giving me a little tug. In a flash, he had me right close. Caging me between his knees, he rested his hands on my hips. "You succeeded," he said simply.

I bit my lip to keep from smiling like a loony girl. "Did we already say hello?" My voice came out breathy, and I thought maybe I sounded ridiculous.

"There's two kinds of hello for you." His smile unfurled slowly, sending my heart into another happy dance and heat sliding like lava through my veins.

I cocked my head to the side, genuinely curious. "What do you mean?"

"There's a regular hello. Then, there's the it's-been-too-many-damn-days-since-I had-a-few-minutes-alone-with-you-and-I-missed-you hello."

His dark eyes softened as he explained this. One hand

shifted on my hip, the backs of his fingers brushing along the dip in my waist as he tugged me even closer before cupping my chin in his palm.

"Oh." That was barely a word, more of a breath and almost a moan. *This* man, *only* this man, had the ability to set my pulse to racing and fiery electricity scattering like sparks through me.

I was trying to be reasonable, trying to do things in a measured, rational way. But that was the thing with Wade. Nothing was measured, nothing was rational. I was beginning to think that all the time I'd tried so valiantly to hold my feelings at bay had been nothing but irrational.

"You've had a busy schedule, and so have I. But I'm free tonight. Actually, just so it's perfectly clear, for you, I'm free every night," he murmured. I could actually feel the gruff edge to his voice skittering over the surface of my skin, goose bumps rising in its wake.

Our teasing conversation had gotten suddenly dead serious. While my heart did cartwheels inside my chest, kicking my ribs with every turn, I stared into his ebullient gaze and tried to breathe, tried to quell the sense of panic welling inside. I was beginning to come to terms with just how much Wade meant to me. And it absolutely terrified me.

Exacerbating my anxiety around it was the fact that I hated not being in control. But I'd had a little chat with myself and promised myself I wouldn't be stubborn and get in my own way. I *did* try to listen to my mother, after all.

Swallowing, I asked, "Even when you're on call?"

He nodded slowly. "Of course. I might have to go out, but there'd be nothing better than coming back to you, darlin'."

Before I could think that through, he was kissing me. The thing about kisses with Wade was he kissed in the absolute best possible way. The moment his lips met mine, my ability to think went completely offline. For me, that was a necessary thing. Thinking generally didn't help me in moments like this.

As he pulled me closer and drew back a whisper, I took a shuddery breath and let it out. There were some things that felt completely right. Kissing Wade was at very top of that list.

Chapter Twenty-Eight

WADE

After a poorly timed interruption from Jackson, who came into the kitchen searching out food, which was quite effective in breaking up my kiss with Dani, I grabbed her by the hand and all but dragged her to her place. When I offered to take her to mine, she shook her head as we walked swiftly through the cold night. The light snow that had fallen the night before crunched under our feet.

"I'll make you breakfast, and I'm sure I have better options than you do," she'd replied.

Just now, she was kneeling in front of me, her gaze holding mine as she leaned forward, her pink tongue darting out to swipe a drop of cum rolling out the tip of my cock. With her eyes still locked with mine, Dani swirled her tongue around the crown, letting out a satisfied hum when I groaned her name.

When she dragged her tongue along the underside of my cock before lightly kissing the tip, the sight the hottest thing I'd ever seen, I laced my fingers in her hair and held on.

"You're gonna make me lose my mind," I bit out as she

swirled her tongue around the tip again, her eyes holding a teasing glint.

"That's the point," she murmured, right before opening her mouth and sucking me in.

Dani was the kind of woman who, once she decided something was going to happen, didn't hold back. Just now, she truly set out to drive me mad, past any boundary of control. With the warm suction of her mouth and her tongue teasing the underside of my cock, my free hand slapped against the door to brace myself. It was the only thing that kept me from collapsing.

When she took me deep, my cock bumping the back of her throat, I lifted my heavy eyelids. With her hand curled around the base of my shaft, and her tongue swirling around the tip as she drew back, the tether on my control snapped. My release hit me abruptly, and she didn't hesitate, catching it all. While I struggled to keep my knees from buckling, Dani gave a satisfied hum as she pulled away. She swiped her tongue at the corner of her mouth to catch a drop of cum glistening there.

Aside from my jeans being unbuttoned, my boxers shoved down, and my T-shirt pushed up, I was fully dressed. Dani straightened, a sly grin curling the corners of her mouth as she assessed me.

"I suppose you could take off your boots now," she teased.

I managed a husky laugh, loosening my grip in her hair as I pushed away from the door when she stepped back. Whether Dani knew it or not, she had all the power here. There might as well have been an invisible cord between us. She moved, and I followed.

Turning, her eyes caught mine over her shoulder. "Boots off," she said, pointing at my feet. "And you need to shower."

"Bossy much?" I chuckled as I turned back. Kicking off my boots as ordered, I hung my jacket up after tucking myself back into my jeans. "So, you think I need a shower, huh? How about you join me?"

Dani put her hands on her hips, surveying me. "Okay."

And so it was that I pressed Dani against the tiled wall in the shower once I'd washed all the mud off of me. Lifting her knee, I sank home, with her other leg curled around my hips.

"That's right, baby. Exactly where I'm supposed to be."

She giggled in between gasps, and it wasn't long before she was crying out, her channel clenching around me as I followed her over the edge again. After we had toweled dry and collapsed in her bed, the pillows propped behind us, I rolled my head to the side, catching one of her damp curls and drawing it out before letting it bounce against her shoulder when I released it.

"So, can we just admit this is an official thing?" I asked, entirely serious.

Dani drew her knees to her chest, curling her arms around them and propping her chin on her hands. "Official?"

I gave her a long look. "Yes, Dani girl. Official. I know you're private—which goes against how nosy you are, by the way—but this isn't just a fling for me."

She chewed the inside of her cheek, her gaze inscrutable. "I want to, but ..."

"But what?" I pushed. "Something really shitty happened and we never got our chance before. Let's take it now."

I held back the words I wanted to say. I was *so* in love with this woman, so gone for her. I thought I'd been on the way to this back in high school, but things are a little weird when you're that young and kind of stupid. Then, everything got all tangled up.

"But I don't want to be everyone's gossip," she finally said, catching one of her curls in her hand and spinning it around her finger.

"Hell, I've been teased about you the whole time I've

been here. Jackson told me the other day he knew it was just a matter of time. With us."

Dani's cheeks flushed and leaned back into the pillows beside me. "I guess it's not like it's not obvious, seeing as Shay and then Jackson caught us in the middle of, um, a moment."

"Is that what it was? A moment?"

Dani smiled slightly as she considered me. "Maybe it was more than a moment." All of a sudden, her eyes widened dramatically. "Oh shit," she breathed.

"What?"

"We forgot to use a condom. In the shower." Her face had gone white.

"Oh hell." Pausing, I collected my thoughts before asking, "Didn't you say you had an IUD? Not that I assumed that meant we wouldn't use condoms."

She nodded jerkily. "I am. I'm kind of uptight about it. It's just ..." She shook her head quickly, her face still pale. "Nothing's one hundred percent."

I reached over to catch her hand, finding it ice-cold.

"Hey, babe," I said, rising up to pull her into my lap. With her a curvy bundle resting against me, I could feel the tension running in little tremors through her. "Let's not panic. Maybe I should go with you to talk to your doctor, so you can find out just how much you need to worry."

I silently swore. Only Dani could make me forget that. I was usually on the spot with a condom. I wasn't about to suggest that perhaps her reaction didn't need to be this strong. I could only imagine how frightening that time had been for her. I had so many questions and wanted to know more, but now wasn't the time.

Dani took several deep breaths, finally looking over at me with a little more color in her cheeks. "I'm sure it's fine." Her gaze searched mine, questions swirling. "Wade, if we're going to be official, how important is it to you to have children?"

Just as before, this question felt so weighted. There was more than a current underneath. It was a riptide I couldn't even see.

I elected to answer cautiously. I didn't want her to worry, and she seemed *really* worried. "Babe, it's not a big deal to me. I wish you would stop fretting."

Dani took a breath, letting it out in a shuddering sigh. "Okay. I'll try."

We sat quietly as she relaxed against me, warm and soft. "For someone who isn't sure you want us to be official, seems like you're skipping ahead a few giant steps with the kids conversation," I murmured.

She lifted her head, her eyes boring into mine. "I guess I'm a little hyper-sensitive about it just because of what happened."

"I get it. It's totally fine with me if we jump ahead. If you told me you wanted to go get married tomorrow, or tonight, for that matter, I wouldn't hesitate." I meant for my words to be a light tease, but when her eyes went comically wide, I added, "Stop looking like that, I was just trying to lighten the moment."

I took it as a total win that she merely rolled her eyes before tucking her head into the curve of my neck.

Chapter Twenty-Nine

DANI

Wade's words played on a loop in my mind over the next few days. As luck would have it, my schedule and his didn't match at all. Although he had said I was welcome at his place anytime, I couldn't quite bring myself to go over there on the nights I knew he was on call when I was working late.

I told myself it was for the best, that we needed time to adjust. In all honesty, my doubts and anxieties were so well-established, they were winning the marathon in my brain. More and more, I was sensing I was the one who'd gone and fallen too hard and fast. I wasn't so sure Wade was where I was on this spectrum of madness.

Late one afternoon, I headed over to the vet clinic to meet with Shay and Valentina. We met together monthly to review numbers and go over accounts together. While Shay handled the management for the rescue program and the vet clinic, I handled everything for the lodge with the exception of the reservations.

I occasionally marveled that I had somehow managed to handle all of it before. It had been haphazard at best. As it was, I was still thanking my stars we had Valentina handling all of the bookkeeping and accounting. I ducked my head down as a blast of icy wind came through the valley. As I walked through the trees between the lodge and the old farm, I looked up and saw Gloria ambling along ahead of me.

The giant pig appeared to hear me. She stopped where she was and looked back. Curling my hand around my laptop bag, I picked up my speed. "Hey, Gloria girl," I said when I reached her side.

Gloria sniffed my knee and leaned her head against my leg. With my gloved fingers, I stroked between her ears and she made snuffling sounds and began to amble along by my side as I hurried the rest of the way to the clinic.

Pausing beside the barn entrance, I glanced down to her. "You headed back to your barn?" I asked. As if she could actually understand my question. I took it as a yes when she gave me a gentle nudge on the knee and continued walking in that direction.

Letting myself through the side door into the barn, I breathed a sigh of relief when the warmth surrounded me. I hurried up the stairs that led to the back hallway in the vet clinic. When I crested the landing, I unzipped my jacket and paused to turn on the Christmas lights back here. Shay had strung them along the ceiling in all of the offices after we'd decorated the reception area.

Only a week and a half until Christmas. My belly fluttered, and I wondered why Christmas elicited thoughts of Wade. As I walked down the hallway, my footsteps loud on the vinyl tiles, my mind spun back to the Christmas before Wade and I had ever even kissed back in high school.

Since I was friends with Wade and his younger sister, they had invited me over that afternoon, after all the family activities had finished. His sister, Piper, was teasing him about some girl she thought he had a crush on. The following day, he fessed up that I was the object of his crush.

"Dani." Valentina's voice punctured my foray to a

memory I'd willfully ignored for years. Looking up, I saw her leaning out of her office door, her brows raised.

"Right here," I said as I strode toward her.

When I reached her, she smiled. "That's the third time I said your name. I was wondering if I should start a fresh pot of coffee," she explained as I stepped through her office door.

"I always say yes to coffee, but thanks for asking," I replied, breezing past her observation that apparently I hadn't heard her say my name twice. Setting my laptop bag down on the round table in the corner of her office, I shrugged out of my jacket and sat down. "Where's Shay?"

"Checking someone out up front. She'll be back in a few minutes," Valentina replied over her shoulder as she prepped the coffee and hit the start button on the pot situated on a small table against the wall by her desk.

Just then, Shay came through the door with her laptop. I was relieved she appeared and temporarily cut off the opportunity for Valentina to follow up on her observation. I didn't like to be caught zoning out, especially not about Wade.

"Oh good," Shay said as she sat down with a flourish. "Thank God you started coffee. Jackson finished off the pot up front."

Valentina smiled as she slipped into a chair. "Since we share the coffee out front with clients, it goes a lot quicker."

"I know," Shay agreed. "Plus, Jackson's a total coffee hog, and Skylar's no slouch."

"How is Skylar working out?" I asked as I pulled up the spreadsheets for the lodge business.

"Great," Shay replied with a vigorous nod, her blonde ponytail swinging back and forth. "I'm so glad Jackson finally hired her. Without Ash, he's up to his eyeballs with his schedule. She can handle a lot of the easier stuff, like shots and so on."

"Any word on when Ash might be back?" I asked.

Shay shrugged. "Honestly, no. She calls, I don't know,

every couple of weeks to check in with Jackson or me. She's supposed to be here for Christmas, but she still hasn't called us with the dates. Not that it matters. She's always welcome. I guess I just worry a little. I know—because of the mess of my life the last few years before I moved back—that she and I weren't in the best of touch. But that was more my fault than hers. This isn't her usual MO to stay out of touch, so it worries me."

Leaning back in my chair, I nodded. "I know. I'm guessing it's her idiot boyfriend."

Valentina glanced between us, her gaze curious. Shay met her eyes and shrugged. "I haven't met the guy. But, Jackson's not a fan. Says he's a total player and has Ash chasing after him."

"That about sums it up," I offered. "I only met him the one time. Ash met him on the rodeo circuit and brought him here for, like, a week or two the summer before last. He was so busy flirting with everybody, there's no way she didn't notice."

Valentina's brow furrowed. "Oh. Well, let's hope for the best."

"Trust me, I'll try to pry some info out of her when she's here. She can't be any more embarrassed than I was. It's not hard to fall into dating a total asshole," Shay commented.

The coffee pot beeped, shifting us off the conversation. "Coffee for everyone?" Valentina asked as she stood.

"Of course," Shay and I replied in unison.

Shay nudged me with her elbow and giggled. "Jinx."

In a matter of minutes, we buckled down and got to work. After two hours of pouring over numbers and making sure everything was as it should be, I tugged on my winter coat to head back over to the lodge.

I left Valentina and Shay behind while they compared options for vet supply companies. Jackson's voice carried down the hallway as he spoke soothingly to an animal. The upper hallway door closed behind me, and the quiet of the barn below enveloped me as I walked downstairs.

My winter boots had soft rubber soles, which was probably the only reason Wade and Lucas didn't hear me coming down the stairs.

Lucas's voice carried up to me. "So, it sounds like things might be getting serious with Dani, huh?"

I froze, curling my fingers tightly around the strap of my laptop bag with one hand and hanging onto the round wooden railing by the stairs with the other as if my life depended upon it. I could hardly breathe, almost leaning forward out of fear I might miss Wade's reply.

Whatever he said initially was masked by the sound of a rake dragging through the dirt aisle between the stalls. What I heard next was loud and clear. "Hard to say. Dani's holding things close. But then, that's how she is."

My mouth fell open. Although I'd known Wade for years, I was still startled by how accurate his observation was.

"What about you though?" Lucas asked next.

Wade's voice was even louder now, so I presumed he'd walked closer to this end of the barn. "I'm not sure. Part of me wants to take things to the next level, but if it's not what Dani wants, then I need to back off."

My breath caught in my throat and a sudden rush of tears pressed hot in my eyes. I blinked rapidly. *Don't you dare start crying here on the stairs.*

I tried to breathe as silently as possible. With the way my heart was pounding and my gut was churning, that was no easy feat.

Lucas said something else I didn't capture, but then Wade's voice carried to me again. "She's freaking out about kids. I want kids. I always have, honestly. Dani definitely went through some stuff, but she's gone from being able to do nothing but give me hell to running hot and cold. I just don't know what she wants."

"You didn't really answer my question," Lucas drawled.

Although I was still fighting tears, I almost laughed. I had noticed the same thing.

At that moment, the door at the top of the stairs opened and I heard Jackson and Shay. With no choice, I resumed walking down. When I stepped off the bottom stair, Wade leaned around the wide archway leading into the barn. "Oh, hey," he said. "I thought I heard Jackson."

I prayed my face didn't give me away. "He's right behind me," I managed, gesturing over my shoulder.

I kept moving, only stopping when Wade lightly caught my elbow. "Hey, what's the rush?" His tone was light.

When I spun back, I collided with his warm dark eyes. For just a moment, the temptation to lose myself in his gaze was almost overwhelming.

"I'm always in a rush," I managed to tease, relieved when Jackson called, "Hey, Wade," from behind me. I jerked away. "I have to get to the kitchen." My words came out in a hurried burst before I almost ran through the door.

———

Christmas decorations were taunting me everywhere. Or at least, that was how it felt. For three days straight, I worked more relentlessly than usual. Up daily before dawn, I walked through the cold darkness to make festive holiday baked goods. We were always short a few staff over the holidays because I never wanted work to interfere with family needs. Instead of running with a thin crew, I even waited tables one evening.

Anything to assist me in my quest to avoid Wade. I didn't know what I'd been hoping for. Since my coping skills of avoidance and denial had been quite successful for years, I hadn't even allowed myself to think much about what I might have wanted for Wade and me, much less allowed something as expansive as hope to walk through the gates to my heart.

I supposed I'd subconsciously hoped for him to at least be able to say I meant something. Rational or not, the tangled past we shared and my not-so-sensible worries about just how important children were to him all twined into the uncertainty I heard in his voice. That uncertainty helped me make the decision I felt necessary. I told myself I could be adult enough not to ice him out of my life, but I just needed a little time before we could be casual and friendly again.

———

I was standing at the reception desk, juggling between phone calls and fielding customers as I escorted them quickly in and out of the restaurant. There was nothing unusual about tonight. With holiday lights glittering all around and festive cheer permeating the restaurant, I was struggling to keep my spirits up.

You're overreacting, my critical voice intoned.

I was as annoyed with myself as I could be. I didn't like feeling like that silly girl who suddenly pinned her hopes on a happily ever after. Especially since I'd been the one to fight so hard against the chemistry between Wade and me.

I was just returning from escorting a family to a table when I felt a sharp, pinching pain in my lower left abdomen. Fear flashed through me.

That was the thing about having something like that almost deadly miscarriage happen. I'd become hyper-sensitive to any little twinge in that zone. I wasn't worried about being pregnant, even in spite of Wade and I forgetting to use a condom that one time. With my IUD, the chances were quite low. But it didn't change my acute sensitivity to anything anywhere near the reproductive area.

It's nothing. It has to be nothing.

I stayed busy enough that I mostly forgot about it until the pain settled in. It wasn't acute, just a deep, achy sensation that wouldn't let up.

I happened to know Wade was on call tonight. I was both relieved and disappointed. I craved the comfort of his embrace, while simultaneously telling myself I was being crazy. I didn't need comfort for anything.

I lay in my bed that night, alone. The pain was still there. I ran my hand over my abdomen. It wasn't cramps, but I suspected something wasn't right.

Chapter Thirty

WADE

For what felt like the thousandth time or so for the last few days, I watched Dani hurry away from me. An errant curl slipped from the knot atop her head and bounced against the side of her neck. I was starting to reach the point of anger with her. She'd gone silent on me again.

I might not be the quickest on the uptake, but I knew damn well she was avoiding me. Quite thoroughly.

Shaking my head, I found Valentina standing by the doorway that led into the back hallway, her gaze tracking Dani's rushed departure.

"What gives?" I asked as I stopped beside her, leaning my shoulder against the wall.

Valentina slid her gaze to mine, quiet for several beats. "I'm not sure," she finally said, her words measured.

Valentina was the kind of person who didn't lie. I knew if she knew what was up with Dani, but Dani didn't want her to talk to me about it, she would say as much.

Tension tightened in my chest a notch further. "Any guesses?"

Valentina's mouth twisted to the side. "Well, I think it has something to do with you. I'm just not sure what."

There went that honesty. "You and me both on that point. Any brilliant suggestions for me?"

Valentina smiled slowly. "Maybe you should try to talk to her."

I threw my head back with a laugh. Shaking my head as I looked her way, I asked, "You ever tried to talk to Dani when she's not in the mood for it?"

Valentina drummed her fingertips on the wall. "No. I can't say I have. Knowing her, it wouldn't be easy." There was a long pause. "But maybe you need to do the difficult thing and ..."

The door opened beside us and revealed Lucas. A blast of cold air gusted through.

"Close the damn door," I said as a few snowflakes blew in with him.

Lucas chuckled, shutting the door quickly behind him. "So, you're telling Wade he's got to do the difficult thing?" he teased as he leaned over and dropped a lingering kiss on the side of her neck.

Valentina smiled up at him as he straightened. "Yes, I am."

Lucas cast me a knowing look. "I've learned she's usually right. Just do whatever she says."

Laughing, I rolled my eyes. "I'm guessing in this case, she's right. Where are you two headed?"

"Home," Lucas replied simply as he slid his arm around Valentina's waist. "Jade's picking up a night shift at the bar because Delilah's out of town, so we need to relieve her of babysitting duties as soon as we can. You ready to go?"

"Of course. Let me get my coat." Valentina stepped out of his embrace and strode down the hallway, returning as she slid her jacket over her shoulders and stuffed her arms in the sleeves.

"Take her advice, man," Lucas said as he held the door for Valentina.

I nodded and watched as they stepped into the snowy darkness, the holiday lights from the lodge illuminating the snow and making it glitter.

Restless, I looked at the clock mounted on the wall toward the front of the kitchen. I guessed Dani would be working at least another few hours. I made a quick decision, figuring it was the only way I was going to catch her alone.

———

I finally heard footsteps coming down the hallway. It was approaching midnight, and I knew just about everybody but the staff who stayed late to clean up the restaurant and kitchen were gone for the night. I prayed those footsteps belonged to Dani. Based on the rapid pace, I surmised they were.

In a few seconds, the door to her office opened and she walked through, her head down as she looked at a notebook in her hands.

"Hey, darlin'," I said from my perch where my hips rested against her desk.

Her head whipped up, her eyes widening with surprise. "Wade, what are you doing here?"

I elected to hew to the simple truth. "Waiting for you."

Her hands slowly lowered with the notebook, and she took a few steps before setting it on the round table. Although only perhaps three feet separated us, I felt like I needed to actually construct a bridge to get to her.

No matter. I was the kind of guy who built things. More than metaphorically, if necessary.

I waited, trying to suss out if she was going to get angry, or if she was going to go cold and quiet. Or, even worse, if she was going to try to play it cool and stay casual.

When her eyes met mine again, I saw pure devastation

there. Although I had no idea what was tumbling about in her mind, I sensed for the first time, I was actually witnessing the pain she experienced that summer.

"Hey, it's okay," I said, straightening and reaching for her hand reflexively.

She shook her head sharply, crossing her arms tightly across her chest. Her position was virtual body armor. "I'm tired, Wade. I don't have it in me to talk tonight."

I took in the shadows under her eyes, the tight lines of her face, and the slight droop to her shoulders. She looked beyond weary, and my heart gave a painful thump.

"We don't have to talk. I just want to say one thing and then I'll go. That okay?" I asked as she stood there in tense silence.

When she nodded, just the littlest bit, I took a deep breath. "Look, I don't know what the hell I did. But I just need you to know where I'm at. I love you. I was halfway in love with you that summer, and then all kinds of things got in the way."

I watched her face carefully. Her cheeks flushed slightly and her eyes widened as her lips parted with a little surprised puff of air. Her arms were still crossed tightly, and I saw her fingertips gripping one of her elbows. Tension vibrated from her, and it made my heart ache a little.

"Okay?" I asked gruffly, stepping a little closer and reaching for her hand.

When she didn't shove me away, I pulled her close. For a moment, she was stiff in my arms, but then she tucked her head against my shoulder and took in a ragged breath.

That was the thing with us—whenever we could touch, everything felt less fraught. Everything felt as if it made sense, like pieces of a puzzle clicking into place.

She mumbled something, but hell if I could hear her. I slid my fingers through her curls. "What was that?"

She lifted her head, leaning back slightly to look at me. "I said, I love you too." Her tone was one of almost protest.

A sense of profound relief washed through me. "Do you now?" I murmured, dusting a kiss at her temple and another on her jaw.

I found her mouth, just as she said, "Mmm-hmm."

I knew we weren't done talking. But, right now, I needed more than words.

Dani seemed to need the same, sighing into our kiss and tugging at my clothes.

It didn't take long for us to leave half of our clothes in a tangle on the floor. After bringing her to one climax with my mouth on her desk, I mapped my way up her body, dropping kisses over the soft curve of her belly and catching a nipple with a light suck. I lifted her knee as I settled my hips into the cradle of hers and sank home in one deep surge.

After what could only be called a quickie in her office, we made our way back to her place for round two. We lay on her bed in a sweaty pile not much later. Rolling over, I pulled her onto my chest with a satisfied sigh. With one hand resting on her sweet bottom, I shifted slightly so we were propped on the pillows.

"Are you planning to keep up the work schedule from hell all the way through Christmas?" I asked.

When she lifted her head, a rueful smile curled her lips. "I'll be busy, but maybe I can make time for you."

I grinned, leaning forward to catch her lips in a lingering kiss. "You gonna tell me what had you avoiding me so thoroughly?"

I tried to keep my tone light. I knew we had to have this conversation one way or another, so I figured we might as well get through to the other side.

She settled her head against my chest again, and I felt her breath gust softly over my skin. "I heard you talking to Lucas in the barn the other day."

"Baby, I talk to Lucas almost every day. You're gonna have to be more specific."

"When he asked you how you felt about me. You were

kind of vague, and I ... I don't know," she said finally, lifting her head and looking in my eyes. "I just got insecure."

"I know you're not a fan of vague, but I guess I didn't really think how you could interpret that."

"Well, you didn't know I was eavesdropping," she replied, her cheeks flushing slightly as she bit her lip.

After a moment, her gaze sobered again.

"What's that look for?" I couldn't say why, but something worried me.

"So, there was that, and that's just my own shit. But then, well, I had a weird pain. I think it's my ovary."

Raw fear bolted through me. "What?"

"It's got to be nothing. I'm just kind of freaky about my body. That made me a little crazy the last few days."

"Does it still hurt?" I asked, looking down toward her belly. As if that would give me any answers.

I was usually steady as a rock with injuries. I was a first responder. I could set bones and do emergency patch-ups and all kinds of stuff. But this had me spinning inside.

"It went away," she insisted, circling her hand on my chest.

Leaning back, I stared at the ceiling and took a slow breath. "Promise me you'll go talk to your doctor," I said when I rolled my head to the side to look at her.

"I'm sure it's nothing," she protested.

"Dani, do it. Please. Do it for me as a personal favor. Also, can you ask her just how freaked out you need to be? I'm all on board with condoms and birth control and what-ever you want, but I'd like to know just how much you need to worry. Because I don't like you worrying."

When I brushed her hair away from her face, she nodded. "Okay."

Chapter Thirty-One

DANI

The paper crinkled under my legs as I rolled up to a seated position. Dr. Sue pushed the stirrups out of the way for me to lower my feet. My bright pink socks looked back at me when I glanced down. "It's still cold in here," I offered.

She looked over her shoulder and grinned. "I know."

After disposing of her gloves, she turned back, leaning her hip against the counter a few feet away. "My guess is, you were ovulating. Sometimes ovulation can cause that kind of pinching, achy pain you described. Both of your ovaries feel exactly the way they should, so I have no reason to do further testing."

"Oh," I said softly, feeling rather foolish.

"I'd rather you come in anytime than work yourself up into a tizzy inside. You had a scary thing happen once, so it's completely reasonable for you to be more sensitive than most to any pain in your reproductive zone."

"Is that what you call it?" I asked with a slight smile.

She shrugged. "That's what it is. Any other questions for me today?"

"One more." Taking a breath, I blurted it out. "So, I have the IUD, but I'm so freaked out about getting pregnant that I'm asking"—I paused long and hard here because I didn't know what word to use to describe Wade—"my boyfriend to wear condoms too. Is that overkill?"

One thing I'd always loved about Dr. Sue was she took every question I threw her way seriously, and she was never dismissive.

Just now, she nodded slowly, her gaze considering. "Here's the thing, the only one hundred percent way not to get pregnant is not to have sex. Or engage in any advanced technology that allows women to get pregnant with other methods, I should add. But an IUD is more effective than condoms at preventing pregnancy. Condoms protect from STDs in addition to pregnancy, so if you're not concerned about that, I would say you're in the clear to have sex with your IUD. It's about as good as it gets for protection. I trust you recall our prior chats about STDs and so on. I won't repeat myself unless you need me to."

I felt my cheeks heat slightly, but I nodded slowly. "I'm not worried about that."

"Is your boyfriend pressuring you to not have sex with condoms?"

"Oh no! He's totally fine with it."

A look of relief passed across her face. "Good to know. I always get concerned when there's pressure around that."

"I guess I was more worried about me overreacting than anything."

"I think you're all set," she said with a smile. "It's a little funny that at your last visit, you were asking about pregnancy, and this one you're making sure your birth control is good enough. I'm getting the impression you're finally dating someone you might be serious about."

My cheeks got hotter. "You could say that."

———

"Yes!" Dawson exclaimed, punching his fist in the air as he spun in a circle.Evie burst out laughing beside him, rolling her eyes as he picked her up and spun her around in his arms.

When he set her down, she shook her head. "You won a stuffed horse."

"Babe, I don't care what I won. I just like to win," Dawson replied with a grin.

I leaned back in my chair, letting my gaze travel around the room. The staff kitchen had been very belatedly decorated for the holidays, with lights strung haphazardly around the ceiling and a giant wreath mounted on the wall above the door leading into the front kitchen. We'd carted extra chairs back here for our last-minute staff holiday party.

Wade stretched his arm across the back of my chair as I glanced in his direction. "Do you want to win something?" he asked, one corner of his mouth curling in a grin and sending butterflies spinning in my belly.

"I certainly don't need to win a stuffed animal," I replied, biting back a smile.

"Oh, come on." Dawson overheard my reply as he sat down beside me, stuffed horse in hand. He had Evie's hand held firmly in his other. "Hey, Lucas!" he called.

Lucas looked up from where he sat on the stool beside the wide baking table. He finished chewing a piece of pizza before replying, "Yeah?"

"This is for Rylie," Dawson said, holding the stuffed horse aloft.

"In that case, go win me a stuffed animal so I can give it to Rylie," I said to Wade.

Wade leaned over, dropping a hot kiss on the side of my neck as he stood. "Anything for you, baby."

As he strode over to a hastily organized contest that involved darts and a basket of stuffed animals, Shay leaned over from the chair just beyond the one Wade vacated.

"Now *that* is a man who is whipped," she teased.

"You think?" I couldn't help but ask. Everything was so fresh with Wade, I was still marveling at how it felt.

"Oh, I don't think, I know," Jackson commented, leaning forward past Shay and giving me a wink.

Chapter Thirty-Two

WADE

Dani walked beside me with her mittened hand clasping mine, the snow crunching under our feet. We were passing by a tall pine tree decorated with holiday lights by the lodge when I gave her hand a little tug and came to a stop.

She looked up at me. "What?"

"Merry Christmas," I said as I reeled her close to me, the lights from the tree casting a silvery glint on her curls as the snow drifted down around us.

"Merry Christmas," she said softly.

The moment felt magical. With the snow glittering in the lights as it fell, and the cold air still around us, the moment felt suspended in time. Leaning down, I brushed my lips across hers, feeling what was becoming a familiar *zing* of electricity spiral through me from where our lips met.

She shivered slightly, and I lifted my head. "Come on." Turning, I gave her hand a little tug, walking swiftly through the trees. I stopped at a branch in the path, glancing down. "Your place or mine?"

Peering up at me, she squeezed my hand and lifted her

shoulder in a shrug. "I don't care. The only thing that matters is you're there."

EPILOGUE

Dani

A year and a half later, or thereabouts

Sweat rolled down my back, and I gritted my teeth as a bolt of pain struck me. "Oh my God! This hurts!"

The friendly nurse, whose name I couldn't recall to save my life, looked over from whatever she was doing at the small cart beside my hospital bed and gave me a sympathetic smile. "Labor usually does. Do you want me to have the anesthesiologist come in?"

Another contraction struck, and I gasped my way through it. When the pain passed, I answered, "I want Wade to get here first."

At that moment, the door to my hospital room swung open. "Just in time," the nurse said with a smile as Wade barreled through the door.

His hair was a mess, sticking up all over his head, and his eyes were wide as he approached the bed. "Are you okay?"

I almost started laughing at his ludicrous question, but another contraction hit me. I closed my eyes as the wave of pain tightened in my lower back and radiated around to my abdomen.

"I think that might've been a dumb question," he said when he reached my side.

I managed to smile as the pain receded. My breath came in ragged heaves and another drop of sweat rolled down my back.

"I was just asking her if she wanted me to call for the anesthesiologist," the nurse said.

Wade leaned his hip against the bed as he reached for my hand, engulfing it in his large, strong grip. "Do whatever you want."

I took another breath, feeling a contraction coming. I was relieved when this one wasn't that bad. "I thought this would be easier," I gasped once I could speak again.

Wade lifted his free hand, brushing my damp curls away from my forehead. "I don't think this is supposed to be easy, babe."

"Fuck natural birth," I muttered after the next contraction gripped me. Rolling my head to the side, I nodded at the nurse. "Anesthesiologist."

I lost all sense of time as the hours passed during that night. I'd gone into labor seven days early while Wade was out on a call. He'd hemmed and hawed about even being on call that close to my due date, but I'd insisted he not do anything different with his schedule. I'd been trying to manage my irrational anxiety about our baby's pending arrival by hewing hard to acting as if everything were just the same.

The moment my water broke, I realized how stupid that was. I'd been utterly terrified when the contractions started, but Wade's arrival eased my fear. I didn't like to lean on anyone, but he made it easy.

During the long hours that followed, labor itself was so consuming, it was impossible to dwell on anything other than what I was doing.

"One more push," Dr. Sue said from where she stood between my feet.

I gripped Wade's hand tightly as I closed my eyes and bore down, an intense burning sensation radiating through my entire body followed by a loud cry filling the room.

"A baby boy. Time of birth, four twenty-two a.m. Do you want to cut the cord, Dad?" Dr. Sue's voice was distant as I collapsed against the hospital bed.

I remembered only fragments of the next stretch of time after that. Wade releasing my hand as he stepped to the foot of my bed, the nurse laying our little baby boy on my chest and belly, and opening my eyes as I looked into my baby's eyes—round and brown, just like his father's.

He went still, little rapid breaths coming in and out of his mouth as we stared at each other. My heart felt as if it were literally going to burst when Wade rested his hand on my shoulder, lowering his head until it was level with mine.

"Well, hello there," he said softly.

―――――

WADE

Dani was sound asleep, her dark lashes curled up against her cheeks. Our little boy was also asleep, nestled in the crook of my arm as I dozed in and out of wakefulness sitting in a chair beside her bed. A nurse kept checking in on us, and the distant sounds outside our room carried on in a strangely comforting rhythm.

I thought I had understood the concept of love. What I hadn't quite comprehended was just how deep the vein of it ran for Dani. When I got the call on my cell that she had gone into labor early and realized I couldn't get to her instantly, sheer panic had gripped me.

Although I had done plenty of reading and knew the odds that she was going to be fine were quite high, it had still been terrifying. But now, the sense of peace that fell over me was so complete, I didn't even know how to measure it.

I heard a rustle and rolled my head to the side in my chair. Dani's eyes flicked open. "Hey," she croaked.

"Hey. Our little guy is doing just great. He's a great sleeper."

Dani's smile was weary. "I bet he's exhausted. It took me sixteen hours to get him out."

With my free hand, I reached up and caught hers in mine. "Wanna hold him?"

"I don't want to wake him up."

Holding her gaze, I released her hand to brush her curls away from her eyes. "How are you feeling?"

"Tired and more sore than I've ever been in my entire life," she said bluntly.

I grinned. "I bet." After a quiet beat, I asked, "You ready for this? Because it just got real. Real fast."

She held my gaze for a long moment before nodding slowly, another tired smile curling her lips. "I'm ready for anything with you."

Thank you for reading Truly Madly Mine - I hope you loved Dani & Wade's story!

Up next in the Swoon Series is Still Go Crazy. Boone is back in town & Grace wants *nothing* to do with him. He might be panty-melting hot, but she can stand the heat. All she has to do is remember how he dumped her.

Boone sets out to fix the biggest mistake of his life— breaking Grace's heart. She isn't about to make it easy for him even if her cat thinks he's awesome.

Grace is strong & sassy, and Boone is all alpha and ready to fight to win her back. Their second chance romance is hot, intense & swoon-worthy.

Keep reading for a sneak peek!

Be sure to sign up for my newsletter for the latest news, teasers & more! Click here to sign up: http:// jhcroixauthor.com/subscribe/

EXCERPT: STILL GO CRAZY

Grace

My ancient cat, Wayne, let out a plaintive meow.

"Seriously?" I countered, turning to glare at Wayne.

Wayne cocked his head to the side before lifting his haunches slightly and settling back down. His only reply was another meow. This time, his annoyance was quite clear.

I eyed the tree from where I stood on the back deck. It was a lovely dogwood situated in the backyard. "Wayne, how the hell did you get up there?"

Although I didn't expect an answer, I was genuinely curious. According to the vet, Wayne was close to blind as a result of his cataracts. He was approaching seventeen years old, so it was surprising he could see anything, much less climb a tree.

I rested a hand on my hip, contemplating my options. "I need to get to work, you know," I called over to him.

Wayne didn't even deign that with a response. My father had gotten Wayne for me when I was thirteen, and Wayne had come to live with me in this duplex after I graduated from college. My parents bought the duplex when they had a brief separation while I was in college. After they reunited, they kept it and rented it out. When my father passed away, my mother deeded the whole place to me.

I'd arranged for a property management company to rent out the other half of the duplex because I hated trying to screen tenants. I wished I knew who'd moved in the day before because I could've used some help at the moment.

With another long look at Wayne on his perch, I glanced at my watch and contemplated if I had enough time to do this. It didn't really matter if I did because I wasn't leaving until Wayne was safely inside.

Wayne meowed again, and I glared at him from the porch. "You're an idiot, you know?"

This wasn't the first time Wayne had climbed into his favorite tree and been unable to get down. I had an excellent view from the deck upstairs. The duplex was built into a sloping hill with the living space on the upper floor with a garage that was nothing more than a glorified storage space on the lower floor. Stepping back inside, I jogged down the stairs and snagged the ladder before walking out into the backyard. I leaned the ladder against the tree and commenced the rescue of my adventurous, geriatric cat.

I climbed to the top of the ladder with my feet firmly hooked into the rungs. I was reaching for Wayne when he meowed and shifted just as I leaned over to get him. In a flash, one of my feet wobbled, I lost my balance, and reflexively grabbed for the closest sturdy branch. Unfortunately, I accidentally kicked the ladder loose when my weight shifted.

"Wayne!" I exclaimed as I found myself dangling from the tree branch. Granted, I was only maybe ten feet in the air, but I didn't really want to drop from this height. Wayne walked closer, leaning his head down to nuzzle my hand. He peered at me, his foggy round blue eyes assessing me.

"You know, Wayne, you can't keep doing this," I said conversationally as I assessed my situation. My only actual option was dropping to the ground.

Just as I was considering whether or not I might break an ankle in the process of doing so, I heard a voice.

"Grace?"

I knew that voice. Oh-so-very well.

My pulse took off at a gallop, and my stomach knotted immediately. Of all the times for Boone Reeves to see me, it just had to be now. I promptly decided I'd rather dive straight to the ground and break my ankle than ask for his help. As soon as I made that decision, I looked down and reconsidered. The grass was just far enough away that if I didn't land well, it would be unpleasant.

More unfortunate than me encountering Boone at this particular moment was the fact that Boone was a rescue kind of guy. Peering over my shoulder, I saw him jogging off the back porch of the duplex.

What the hell is he doing here?

Boone stopped at my feet and glanced up. Without even asking, he quickly propped the ladder against the tree and climbed it, reaching for my hand.

"Come on," he said. "I'll get you down."

"Boone, that ladder can't hold both of us."

"Sure it can. Come on, Grace."

Wayne meowed loudly and then started purring. My cat was fucking purring at the sight of my ex. The man who all but threw my love in the trash.

Boone's face cracked with a grin. "Nice to see you again, Wayne." His gaze swung back to me. "Grace, your arms are shaking. Let me help you."

My arms *were* shaking, and my hands were tired. I didn't want help from anybody, most adamantly *not* Boone. But I prided myself on being a smart girl.

Biting back a sigh, I shifted slightly, and Boone wrapped his arm around my waist. The feel of his strong, steady touch was like a live wire, electrifying my entire body.

I had successfully avoided too much contact with Boone

for almost a year now. Without a doubt, being this up close and personal with him was a special kind of hell.

"Boone." His name just slipped out, my voice sounding frayed. I was getting anxious as he tugged me a little closer.

"Grace, I've got you. I promise."

The thing was, I believed him. Boone wouldn't drop me. He might've once kicked my love to the curb as though it had never mattered, but he wouldn't let me fall. Truth be told, he wouldn't let anyone in my situation fall. He was strong and resourceful, oozing with that save-any-damsel-in-distress vibe.

I stopped resisting, and Boone pulled me even closer. I finally let go of the tree branch completely, both out of resignation and sheer tiredness. My arms were shaking and a strange tingling sensation was taking over. I made a mental note to start doing pull-ups, almost embarrassed at how poor my upper body strength was.

With one hand on the ladder, Boone held me close as I fumbled to get my feet on the rungs.

"I gotcha," he said.

The raspy vibration of his voice, so close to my ear, sent an inconvenient shiver chasing over my skin. In a matter of seconds, we were on the ground. I stepped back abruptly, my legs almost giving out. I didn't know if my shakiness was from hanging onto the branch ...or from getting too close to Boone.

My cheeks were hot, but I willed myself to look at him. I wasn't going to be a coward. I met his gaze head-on, trying and failing to take a deep breath. My body was in an all-out war with my mind.

Boone was everything I remembered and more. It wasn't that I hadn't seen him recently. It was more that I hadn't allowed myself more than a passing glance. The young man he'd once been had been honed into much *more* of a man. Tall with a rangy build, his shaggy dark blond hair was rumpled with the ends brushing his shoulders. He moved with an unconscious grace and was all lithe, lean muscle.

Boone looked at me, his dark chocolate gaze coasting over me, warm and concerned. "You okay?" he asked.

I swallowed and nodded. "Yeah. Thanks for that."

He gestured up toward Wayne. "I'm guessing you were trying to get Wayne down."

Butterflies had taken up residence in my belly, an unsettled bunch of them. Wrapping my arms around my waist, I gripped my elbows tightly, trying to find an anchor inside the storm of emotions buzzing through my body.

With Boone's eyes holding mine, the beginning of a grin teasing at the corners of his mouth, I felt as if I had stepped through a window in time—back to our senior year of high school when Boone was my boyfriend. We spent many afternoons together, and Boone had been endlessly amused by Wayne's antics.

"Yeah," I finally managed to reply, the word coming out ragged.

"I'll get him." Boone turned, climbing the ladder before I could even respond. In another moment, I heard him murmuring to Wayne as my cat nestled into the crook of his arm, staying put as if he were a well-trained, obedient cat.

"Where should I take him?" Boone asked once he was standing on the ground in front of me again. Wayne, the disloyal cat that he was, was purring up a storm now and rubbing his chin against Boone's shoulder.

I had to unstick myself and climb back through that window in time to the present. "Right this way," I said, turning and almost running into the house. Coming to a skidding stop on the back deck, I looked up at Boone. "I can take him."

Wayne, as if he knew what I meant, meowed and burrowed deeper into Boone's arms. When I tried to reach for him, Wayne was having none of it, shifting away from me and burying his face against Boone. Boone chuckled.

With a sigh, I gestured for Boone to follow me inside. "Come on up."

The downstairs of the duplex contained a shared entryway and two separate staircases that led to the upstairs on each side. I had a sickening feeling that the property management company had rented it to Boone.

Opening the door upstairs, I held it as Boone walked through. At that point, Wayne leaped out of his arms and immediately climbed into his small bed on the windowsill.

"Well, thanks again," I said as I turned back to Boone.

This was supposed to be the point where Boone took the hint and left. He didn't.

Cocking his head to the side, his gaze swept over my face. "I'm just now realizing that you're my neighbor," he said softly.

BOONE

Grace Lakes stood before me, her mesmerizing silver eyes flashing and her chin lifting with a stubborn tilt. My entire body felt like an antenna tuned to one frequency—Grace.

I wanted a reckoning with her, but I hadn't counted on it being like this.

"You rented the other half of the duplex?" she asked, each word enunciated clearly in that soft, crisp tone of hers.

Most people who had a Southern accent had words with round edges, where everything kind of sloughed off slowly, moving like honey. With Grace, she had the twang, but her enunciation was so precise and clear. It was strangely endearing to me—just like the first time I fell for her—and now, knowing just how easily I'd fallen under the spell of this woman once before.

As I stared at her, I realized I hadn't actually heard her voice since I'd moved back to Stolen Hearts Valley last year. I'd seen her plenty of times—every single time was a yank on the string attached to my heart.

I nodded slowly, waiting for her to flee. After all, that's what she always did when we were anywhere in the same vicinity for the last year.

During the moments I took her in, Grace tucked her arms around her waist again, her shoulders curling inward. She bit the corner of her lip. I wanted to lift my thumb, to smooth the furrow on her brow and cup her cheek.

I didn't realize I had actually done what I was thinking until I was standing right in front of her, my thumb resting over the rapid flutter of her pulse along the side of her neck.

Her breath drew in sharply. I stared into her smoky, gorgeous eyes. I didn't realize I'd been holding my breath until she spoke.

"Boone."

The sound of my name coming from her lips was a fiery jolt to my heart

"Yeah, sugar?"

The endearment slipped out. I could feel the tension vibrating from Grace, a subtle tremor running through her.

We stood like that, frozen in place with our eyes locked together. Grace's eyes were like one of those afternoons when the sky couldn't decide if it planned to riot with a storm or let the clouds blow by.

Her smoky gaze flashed in shades of silver. All the while, I held my breath.

Just as I had reached up to cup her cheek without thinking, so did I dip my head and brush my lips across hers. Sensation shot through me, so electric was the feel of her lips under mine.

Grace gasped, literally jumping away from me. "I can't!"

Angling my head to the side, I eyed her carefully. "I don't see why not, Grace. I've missed you. So damn much."

She stared at me, her lips parted slightly and her shoulders rising and falling with her rapid breaths.

"How can you say that?" she countered as a look of pure devastation passed over her face. It took all I had not to walk over and pull her into my arms and explain the whole fucking mess. I wanted to make her listen, to make her understand.

Yet, I knew Grace. I knew her *so* well. She hated to be pushed and only strengthened her defenses when anybody put pressure on her.

Closing my eyes, I took a breath and nodded as I opened them. "Just let me explain what happened."

"Please just go." Her words were raw and frayed around the edges. Her eyes were bright, and I knew I saw the glitter of unshed tears. "Just go," she repeated, this time her voice more forceful.

Wayne took that moment to meow loudly. Mentally wrestling, I debated whether to stay. Just then, my cell phone rang with the distinct warning tone for Stolen Hearts Valley Emergency Response Team. I was on call, and that meant I needed to get going. "I'll go, but I want to try to talk soon. Please."

Grace lifted her chin, the muscles in her jaw tightening. "I don't know what the hell there is to talk about."

I closed the distance between us, cupping her chin lightly. "You know damn well there is. If there wasn't, you wouldn't have managed to avoid getting anywhere near me for most of the year since I came back. I know I fucked up and didn't handle things well, but you never even gave me a chance to explain. I won't take a chance now, but it's coming."

At that, I bent low once more and brushed my lips across hers again, almost craving the hot jolt it gave my system. I recognized the answering flare of desire in Grace's eyes when I lifted my head. Without a word, I walked past her and jogged down the stairs as my phone blared again.

———

Coming February 2020!
    Still Go Crazy

If you love hot, small town romance, take a visit to Willow Brook, Alaska in my Into The Fire Series. Check out Burn For Me - a second chance romance for the ages. It's FREE on all retailers! Don't miss Cade & Amelia's story!

Go here to sign up for information on new releases: http://jhcroixauthor.com/subscribe/

FIND MY BOOKS

Thank you for reading Truly Madly Mine! I hope you enjoyed the story. If so, you can help other readers find my books in a variety of ways.

1) Write a review!
2) Sign up for my newsletter, so you can receive information about upcoming new releases & receive a FREE copy of one of my books: http://jhcroixauthor.com/subscribe/
3) Like and follow my Amazon Author page at https://amazon.com/author/jhcroix
4) Follow me on Bookbub at https://www.bookbub.com/authors/j-h-croix
5) Follow me on Instagram at https://www.instagram.com/jhcroix/
6) Like my Facebook page at https://www.facebook.com/jhcroix

Swoon Series
    This Crazy Love
    Wait For Me
    Break My Fall
    Truly Madly Mine
    Still Go Crazy - coming February, 2020!
Into The Fire Series
    Burn For Me
    Slow Burn
    Burn So Bad
    Hot Mess
    Burn So Good
    Sweet Fire
    Play With Fire
    Melt With You
    Burn For You
    Crash & Burn
Brit Boys Sports Romance
    The Play
    Big Win
    Out Of Bounds
    Play Me
    Naughty Wish
Diamond Creek Alaska Novels
    When Love Comes
    Follow Love
    Love Unbroken
    Love Untamed
    Tumble Into Love
    Christmas Nights
Last Frontier Lodge Novels
    Take Me Home
    Love at Last
    Just This Once
    Falling Fast
    Stay With Me

When We Fall
Hold Me Close
Crazy For You
Just Us
Catamount Lion Shifters
Protected Mate
Chosen Mate
Fated Mate
Destined Mate
A Catamount Christmas
The Lion Within
Lion Lost & Found

ACKNOWLEDGMENTS

This one goes out to every woman who's made it through to the other side of an unexpected loss. So many stories are carried in silence, and Dani's was one of those. Know that you are never alone even if it feels like it sometimes.

I'm always grateful to my editor for making sure I give my characters their best stories. Terri D. not only proofreads like a champ, but she's such a fabulous support to me and many other authors.

Many thanks to my ARC readers who make sure my book babies go out with their best foot forward - Janine, Beth P., Terri E., Heather H., & Carolyne B.

To my family for being there, and to my dogs for reminding me every single day what unconditional love means.

xoxo
J.H. Croix

ABOUT THE AUTHOR

USA Today Bestselling Author J. H. Croix lives in a small town in the historical farmlands of Maine with her husband and two spoiled dogs. Croix writes contemporary romance with sassy women and alpha men who aren't afraid to show some emotion. Her love for quirky small-towns and the characters that inhabit them shines through in her writing. Take a walk on the wild side of romance with her bestselling novels!

Places you can find me:
jhcroixauthor.com
jhcroix@jhcroix.com

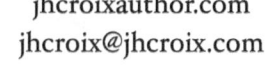 facebook.com/jhcroix

 twitter.com/jhcroix

 instagram.com/jhcroix

www.ingramcontent.com/pod-product-compliance
Lightning Source LLC
Chambersburg PA
CBHW050514190726
48284CB00003B/803